'I am Daniel Tahi.'

A Telesa Novella.

By

Lani Wendt Young

ISBN-13:978-1481888721

ISBN-10:148188722

Due to mature themes, sexual content and language – this novella is recommended for readers 17+. Parental discretion is advised.

DEDICATION

To all the Daniel Fans.

Thank you for believing in the possibility of a boy like Daniel Tahi.

ACKNOWLEDGMENTS

To all the readers of the Telesa Series:

Thank you for keeping me company on the writing journey. Your enthusiasm, excitement and love for Leila and Daniel's story has helped to fuel the writing fire. Each of you has helped to take this Pacific tale to a global audience, to places I never imagined it would go.

Faafetai tele lava.

1

It was supposed to be the best year of his life. Or at least a year to make up for the sorrow and struggle of the one before it. He was back at school after taking a year off when his grandfather got sick. Head prefect of the most prestigious school in Samoa. Captain of the First XV rugby team and already on the international talent scout radar, having turned down not one, but two rugby scholarships to New Zealand. He was on target to win the Science Trophy, Mathematics Prize and the Samoa Observer Award for Debate. Not to mention Best All Round Achiever for the year. Business was slowly but surely recovering from the shock of losing his Grandfather. He had been able to meet project deadlines with the help of a capable work team and they had just secured two fencing contracts which would carry them through for at least six months. Yes, everything was going according to plan.

And then out of all the English classes on the island – she had to walk into his. Leila Folger. Or – as he named her in his head, **#AngryGirl**. With a bold caps hashtag. She walked into his life with her sour expression and even more sour attitude, carrying the accumulated weight of a lifetime worth of hurts - looking for a target to hurl her venom at. And he unwittingly volunteered for the job, by opening his big debate-master mouth in Ms Sivani's class.

Compiled here are some insights into Daniel Tahi. What was he really thinking at key points in the last turbulent few months?

****

Sometimes, I wish Leila and I had never met.

Before we met, I knew who I was. Where I was going. The path I walked had a sure foundation. Now? I see that the world I once knew - veiled many secrets. Now, there are things in me that I don't even recognize. They tell me that a telesa's power is birthed with them. But is that really true? All my life, I felt nothing for the sea but hatred. All my life, the sea cared nothing for me. Until I met Leila. Until her fire burned me, in more ways than one. Would I be vasa loloa if I hadn't met her? Now, I don't know what to feel. They tell me my mother worshipped the ocean. And in the end, it took her life. They tell me my father shared her love for its mysteries. But in the end, even that wasn't enough to make him stay. Now, the ocean speaks to me - and I don't want to answer. How can I be a son of the ocean when the ocean took my birthparents from me?

Yeah, sometimes, I wish we had never met. Don't get me wrong - I love her. After all we've been through. All we've endured together. My life's path is inextricably linked with her's. She's fanua afi and I'm supposed to be this vasa loloa thing. Everything tells me we are bound by something greater than ourselves. But there is a finality about it that suffocates me sometimes. Drowns me.

Would I love her this way if we weren't telesa?

All I ever wanted was to make her smile. That day seems so long ago now. An English debate show-down, a hostile girl that hated me even before she met me. It all started because I wanted to make her smile...

And now, here we are. For a smile - I love a fire goddess who can incinerate me with a thought. For a smile - I have put my grandmother's life in danger. For a smile - I'm supposed to be some hero in a screwed up Pacific legend. What guy likes to find out that his girlfriend was 'foretold' in a prophecy? How does it feel? I'll tell you - it sucks. Those epic love stories that live on for generations? They're always tragic tales of doom. Yeah, we remember them forever because the two lovers always end up DEAD. Maybe, I don't want epic. Maybe, I want Leila but I just want 'regular' and normal. You know - boy meets girl. Fireworks. Sparks. Light. Laughter. Love stuff. Will we or won't we... A touch. Her lips on mine. Skin. Heat. A song that only you two can hear.

Is it so wrong to want less than what we have?

But even these questions are a stupid waste of time. Because all the wondering in the world won't change the facts. Because I **do** love her. I **am** vasa loloa. We **are** both telesa. And right now - there is a psycho bitch telesa called Sarona who wants to kill us.

Whether I like it or not, I'm pretty much stuck with EPIC...

So how did it all start? What did I think of Leila when I first saw her? Did I think she was breathtakingly beautiful the first moment I laid eyes on her? No. Did I fall madly in love with her on that first day we met? No....

2

We're having rugby training on the center field before school starts when Maleko nudges me. "Hey, new girl."

I look. Hell, everybody looks. That's how tight SamCo is. I mean there's only four hundred students in the school so anybody new doesn't stay unknown for very long. So yeah, I look over at this girl in the obviously new bright orange and yellow uniform, walking up the driveway with her schoolbag over one shoulder. She's scowling. That's the only word I can think of to describe her face. Most new students look a little wary, sometimes afraid, nervous. But this one? No, she just looks angry. From the expression on her face – the thick dark eye brows, the furrowed brow, the determined set of her jaw – to her rigid posture and tightly clenched fists. The way she walks across the campus with her entire body tensed as if she expects someone or something to attack her at any moment and she is ready for it. She's angry, ready to fight and she wants everyone to know it. She looks over to the rugby field in our direction and she even looks angry to see us.

Maleko whistles, “Sheesh, what’s her problem?”

I shrug, suggest, “I don’t know. Maybe she finds your naked chest offensive? I know I do.”
Maleko swings a casual left hook at me which I duck easily. The others laugh and we all move back to scrum formation. The angry new girl is forgotten.

Until the next day. When I walk into Ms Sivani’s English class and there she is. Sitting next to Simone. And staring. At me. This time, it’s her eyes that catch me. Deep set, ember eyes that are scrutinizing me as if she wants to burn holes in me with her laser beam vision or something. *Great, the angry new girl wants to kill me. And we haven’t even met yet.* For one crazy minute, I have this urge to poke my tongue out at her. To try and tease a smile out of her. I don’t know why, but I want to make this girl laugh. Or at least let go of some of that fury that she seems to be struggling to hold in check. I smile at her. Willing her, asking her with everything I have – to smile back.

It doesn’t work. She just looks angrier. And looks away. *Oh well. It was worth a try.*

Ms Sivani is in fine form. She likes to challenge us, have us ‘push the envelope’, telling us that we’re lazy, complacent students who need to walk on the wild side of the intellectual stimulation wire. She puts the debate topic up on the board and gets us all started on a free-for all debate. One of her favorite activities. That’s when I first find out *her* name.

That's when 'Angry New Girl’ becomes ‘Leila’.

Maleko kick-starts the debate. Of course. Ever the performer, he has everyone laughing. I give him the required hi-five when he’s done. “Nice one.”

He preens, commenting loudly “Just making sure my new *fui*, my new chick, gets a taste of what I have to offer. The complete package. I'm not just a pretty face." He strikes a pose, 'a Professor in deep contemplation' stance. Which I have to go ahead and ruin.

"Does Mele know your pretty face is checking out a new *fui*?"

He gives me an aggrieved look, "Uso, bro that hurts. Why you gonna go and stab me like that?"

"Just reminding you of the status quo brother." I'm only half-joking. Behind her pouty lips and bite-me eyes, Maleko's girlfriend Mele is a cold stone witch who doesn't have a shred of fun in her. Or niceness for that matter. I can't figure out how two such completely different people can be dating. I throw the new girl a quick glance, wondering how she's reacting to Maleko's humor. Sometimes the new ones from overseas don't get it and instead get reactionary. She's looking right at me. With that intense burning stare. Is that her angry face? Or just her regular face? I grin. Heck, what else am I supposed to do?

Nothing. No change. *Riiiighht.*

Suvinia's up next, adding a bit of seriousness to the exercise. And when she's done, my team decides it's time to put me on the spot. Chanting. *Daniel, Daniel, Daniel.* Maleko shoves at my shoulder. "Come on man, your adoring fans are calling for you."

Yeah, here we go. Debating is my next most favourite thing to rugby. Word-master skills. My grandfather always told me that a man who could master his words could master the world. He'd always been a man of few words so it had always seemed to me, a funny thing for him to say. But when my friends were clued to their Xboxes and jamming to MTV specials, my grandparents had me memorizing sections of Shakespeare. The Bible. Keats. Wordsworth. My grandfather had been big on poetry. Don't ask me why.

I stand, smile at the team to quiet them down and get started. First thing on the agenda, "My fellow orators, our ever stunning and wise judge, Ms Sivani, ours is a society plagued by a relentless array of social ills. Drug abuse. Unemployment. Youth crime and delinquency. Not to mention a vast array of non-communicable diseases like diabetes, obesity, high blood pressure, kidney disease. And who do we have to thank for these? Our Western neighbors. Those who come here bearing gifts but they are gifts we should never have accepted. Why, from the very first Western visitors who came here seeking to pillage our land of its natural resources to those countries who give us money – just so that we will support them during international proceedings – we have been fighting a losing battle with our Western neighbors. There can be no doubt that foreign aid is a plague on our beautiful island nation. "

"There's a saying – there's no such thing as a free lunch. Well, Samoa has been well and truly overeating on supposed 'free' lunches, breakfasts, and dinners for too long!"

The class erupts, like I knew it would. I am the master of working the crowd. (If I do say so myself.)

"Let's take an example, one of these supposed aid organizations – the US Peace Corp. They come here to volunteer, but really, aren't they here to disseminate their foreign ideas and values? To convince us of their supremacy in all things?"

I'm on a roll now as I move on to ripping apart other volunteer organizations and then side-tracking to criticize the impact of "intermarriage" on the "purity of our Samoan culture."
Since most of us are a motley assortment of blended Samoans, *afakasi* mixtures - I know that will spark lots of laughter, and I'm right. I'm the only one in the room with Tongan in me though, which always makes for good ammunition whenever the boys are kidding around – I get a lot of horse and dog jokes. (And only Samoans and Tongans will know what I'm talking about…) I had figured out long ago that debating was half acting skill and so, I put on my sad face as I discuss the decay of traditional values due to the country's increased "infiltration" of foreign influence via aid. The cherry on top is my closing statement "Where is the pride and purity of our Samoa? Take a look around these days, we're surrounded by mixed-up mongrels!"

Cheers and shouts and mass laughter. Even though I've gone seriously off topic, I know that Ms Sivani has enjoyed the spectacle because she's battling to contain a smile. I half-bow to the crowd and yeah, I'll admit it, I'm ready to hi-five my own awesomeness. Until I catch sight of the Leila girl. If I thought she looked mad before, it's nothing compared to the toxic expression on her face now. If looks could kill, I would be lasered right through. *What the hell?* There's no mistaking it. There is something seriously wrong with this chick.

And then I'm in trouble. Because she jerks her chair back with a vicious shove, leaps to her feet and rips into me. "What absolute rubbish you're spouting. Not only do your remarks reek of flawed logic, but they also border on outright racism. How dare you pass judgement on volunteers and organizations that dedicate their lives to serving others. Just who in hell do you think you are?" It's the first time I hear her speak. Her voice is pitched lower than most girls and her American accent is chunky thick like peanut butter. She's so mad that every word is spat with poison. Drawn to her full height with fury, this girl is tall. Really tall. She's pointing her finger at me and even her big thick eyebrows are mad at me. The class is in a state of frozen shock. Nobody has ever seen me get blazed out like this. It's kind of funny. Because this girl can't be serious…can she? This is a joke, right?

But she keeps going. Clawing at me with words like 'racist bigot' and telling me I 'carve chasms of hatred' and 'ignite conflict' everywhere. Is she for real? She can't possibly be for real. Surely she must know I was kidding around? Hasn't she ever heard of sarcasm? Irony? Humor? Finally she's all screamed out. She's breathing hard. She sits down and it's my turn. I know. I'll make it clear that this is supposed to be fun. Give her another chance to get the joke. I take my time. Okay, and yeah maybe I play a little to the audience. Because I'm racing through possible responses in my head. Classic debate technique. Fake out the enemy. I smile, pose, pause, run a hand through my hair. The class are used to it. They encourage it. Simone fakes a dramatic sigh of appreciation, playing along with my routine – and then ruins it by mouthing a swear word at me from the back where Ms Sivani can't see him.

"She wounds me!" Hand on my heart. I'm pulling no punches here. Ok, ok, I've upped my performance game for the sake of the new girl. She doesn't look impressed with my playacting though. That glare says, I HATE YOU WITH A PASSION. I do my thing. Winning Ms Sivani over as I always do with unrestrained charm. And the class loves it. Maleko makes a gagging face at me when I end with a grand bow to the audience. Laughter. I sit back down, humbly acknowledging the energetic cheering.

They don't call me the Debate Master for nothing.

She is silent for the rest of the debate. I watch her discreetly. She's still not bending. She's still mad as hell. You can see it in the straight line of her back and those eyebrows that are scrunched up extra thick. I feel a little sorry for her. She is new after all. She can't know how we roll with our debates. That they're usually a free-for-all laugh fest. And everyone gets ripped on. No worries. I'll sort it out after class.

When the bell rings, I go after her. She's walking fast. Angry and fast. I push through the others. "Hey, wait up Leila is it? Wait!"

I know she can hear me but she's pretending not to. I want this fixed today. I have to grab hold of her backpack. "Leila, hang on a minute. Please."

She stops, turns. She's not smiling. "Yes?"

Maleko butts in. "Great debate…" He asks her where she comes from. Good because I was wondering the same thing.

She makes a deliberate point to look at him, letting us know that she's speaking to HIM and HIM only. And not to the jerk who just pissed her off big-time. "The States. Washington D.C. Well, Maryland really. I'm here for the summer holidays to visit my aunt and uncle."

At least she's talking to us. I give her my bestest smile. Friendly and fun. That's me. Mr Fun Friendliness. "Great, welcome to SamCo. I just wanted to say, nice debating. And I hope you didn't take any of it personally. Are we okay?"

Direct and straight for the humility jugular. She can't deny my apology, right?

Wrong. She can. Her face shuts down. "No. We aren't. You know some of us are products of exactly that exploitative union you referred to…" She goes on some more, repeating my words back at me like they're reverse missiles. And yeah, coming from her like that – they do sound a little harsh. I realize then that she thought I meant it. The realization is like a king-hit to the chest. Only a complete ass**** would say that stuff – and mean it.

She thinks I'm a complete ass****.

For some unknown, undefinable reason - I don't want her to think I'm a complete ass****.

But it's too late. She's gone. Pushing through the crowd. Striding away down the hall. Maleko whoops with surprised laughter. "Awww man, crash and burn!" He claps me on the shoulder, "She hates you." He's not sympathetic at all. I frown after him as he walks off, still laughing. What the hell am I going to do?

Someone exclaims next to me, "What a bitch!" It's Simone. He's got his hands on his hips and he's quivering with outrage. "Leave her to me. I'll fix her."

His face leaves me with no doubts just how he's going to 'fix' the new girl. The knife of guilt twists a little deeper. If Simone puts her on his hate-list then #AngryGirl's chances of ever making any friends here are totally shot. And it will be my fault. I grab hold of Simone's shoulder just as goes to flounce away. "Wait. Do me a favour, can you look out for her? Please?"

Simone gives me a look of outrage. "Are you nuts? Why would I do that? She's not my type at all. Did you see her hair? And those butch eyebrows?" A shudder.

"Look, she doesn't know how we roll here. She thought I meant what I said back there in the debate. She's really upset. Can you talk to her? Explain I was kidding?"

He narrows his eyes at me, "What does it matter to you how she feels?"

I can't lie to Simone. He knows me too well for that. I lean in close, keep my words low. "I don't want her to think I'm a jerk. That's all."

A dramatic sigh and roll of his eyes. "Fine. I'll talk to her. But you owe me." He walks away after Leila, snapping at people to get out of his way.

Simone and me, we go way back. I've known him since grade school when his name was Simon. We first bonded over jam sandwiches. Simone's mother used to send him to school with a full-packed lunch. Sandwich, fruit and cookies. In a Hannah Montana lunchbox. Which didn't go down too well with some of the other boys who came to school with no lunches from *their* mothers. The day Mean Willie grabbed Simone's sandwiches and stood on them in the dirt was the first time I ever got sent to the Principal's office for fighting. The first time Mama and Papa were called in to the school to discuss my 'troubling behaviour.' At first they looked mad but when we got home, Papa took me for a long walk on the beach and I had to tell him what happened. When he got the full story, he clapped a hand on my shoulder, looked me straight in the eyes and told me he was proud of me. "Son, you did the right thing. Standing up for others who need your help takes courage. You're only seven but already you're bigger, stronger and faster than lots of other boys your age. If you work hard I know you will have a great future in rugby if you want to. Right now, it's important to use that strength and those talents for good things and never pick on children smaller than you like what those boys at school did today. You keep looking out for that boy Simon, okay? " He paused and stared out over the blue lagoon for a moment before he continued, "And if, one day, other talents, other gifts from somewhere out there," he waved a hand in the vague direction of the white surf crashing on the distant reef, "come to you then remember – you are to use them to help people. Not hurt them."

Papa was a man of few words, which is why that somewhat puzzling speech was one I have never forgotten. Even if I didn't understand it all.

Me and Simone remained friends right through Primary and Intermediate school. He didn't ever need a bodyguard back-up once we reached high school though, because he came into his own and embraced his feminine side. He started calling himself 'Simone.' Simon was the quiet, shy boy who cried when bullies stole his lunch. Simone was the feisty and fierce fa'afafine who could outwit, outplay and humiliate anyone with fast-talking sarcasm if they dared to mess with him. He also had a rapport with many of the girls that most of the boys envied.

If Simone couldn't calm Leila down – then nobody could.

****

I'm on my way home after training when I get Simone's text.

I fixed it.

Three simple words that have me buzzed. I tell myself it's because I don't want a new student to feel unwelcome. It's my civic duty as Head Prefect to make sure Leila Folger has help settling in. That's all it is. I really don't care otherwise.

3

It's the next day and I'm looking out for her. But pretending I'm not. (If you know what I mean.) But only because I'm curious. How will she react when she sees me? Will I still get the hate-fest? What's she like when she's nice? Happy? It should be interesting…

I get called out of class for prefect stuff. I'm on my way to the staffroom when I hear Maleko's distinctive shout. He's on the field with his class at Physical Education. Mr Otele has got them all running laps in the blazing hot sun. Well, Mr Otele is *trying* to get them to run laps in the blazing hot sun. Most of them are walking now, dragging their feet, complaining. I'm laughing, trying to catch Maleko's attention so I can rub it in that I'm strolling along in the shade while he's killing himself out there. Especially because there's a girl in the lead, powering along with long, sure strides while he struggles to catch up. Who is she? The girl rounds the curve of the oval and I see her face clearly. It's #AngryGirl.

Daaayuuum, the girl can run. I'm full-on staring now. Surprised. I can't drag my eyes away from her. Her thick braid hangs down her back to her waist. It sways back and forth as she runs with a single-minded intensity, focused on the track in front her. In the skimpy orange sports uniform skirt, her legs are the most obvious thing about her. They go on forever. And they are very obviously, most distinctly, incredibly impressively NOT Samoan girl taro-legs.

They are legs that belong on a billboard cover model. Not a hostile American afakasi import. #AngryGirl running is a girl worth staring at…

I've got teachers waiting for me though, so I get moving. But it's not easy to shake the image in my head. Of a tall, intense, warrior-woman running with powerful ease under a golden-blue sky.

****

The weeks pass. I decide to put #AngryGirl out of my mind. (The fact I have a special nickname for her is a sign of how well I'm sticking to my decision…) I do have a plan for this year after all. It's simple. Work my ass off in the classroom, on the field and in the workshop. No distractions. No excuses. My schedule is crazy with rugby training and school. I'd been Head Prefect last year when I had to quit school one month in. I hadn't wanted to take on the position again this year but the teachers had other ideas. And Mama had insisted I accept because "it will be useful for your scholarship applications." If you knew my grandmother you would know that one does not argue with her.

So yeah, for my final year at SamCo, girls are a distraction I don't need. Especially angry ones with too much attitude.

So why was I keeping Leila Folger on my radar? I couldn't explain it. I kept it on the down-low though. Never reacted or commented when Maleko and the others talked about her. Critiqued her. Made fun of her slouched walk, or the way she gave everyone the hate stare. I watched on the sly when he joked with her at lunchtime, trying his best to tease a smile out of her, crack the ice shield she wore 24-7. No, I never paid attention. Not really.

Okay, so maybe I did ask Simone about her every now and then. Just a casual few questions. Stuff about where she was from. What was she like. Stuff like that. And Simone gave me the knowing smirk and exasperated sigh, because he always knew when I was full of it. But it was okay. Because it was Simone and I could trust him.

"Why does she always look so angry?" Does she have a boyfriend? Is the question I really want to ask. But won't.

"She already graduated high school in America and she's pissed off that she has to be back in sixth form again." He pauses and stares pointedly at the kekepua'a pork-bun I'd bought for my lunch. A clear signal. I hand it over and he fake exclaims, "For me?! Thank you so much daaahling. You're too kind." He takes a few bites with great relish, before continuing. "She was born here but her Dad took her to America when she was a baby so this is kind of her first time. She's staying with an aunty. She's got no other family. No friends." A frown of distaste. "And she really needs to pluck her eyebrows. Wax her face. And maybe start wearing a push up bra."

I can do without the Extreme Makeover details. I press for more of the stuff I want to know. "Why is she here? How long is she staying?"

A shrug. "I still haven't been able to get her to tell me what she did to have her palagi aiga exile her to our beautiful rock." A sly look. "She listens to some weird stuff on her iPod. Like you."

Aha, this is a nugget of info that I can work with. "Like what?"

Simone waves a hand airily. "White people sounds. Crap like Coldplay. The Script. And U2." His face scrunches up in puzzlement. "But she knows all the words to Eminem's songs. What is up with that?!" Simone is a disciple of Beyoncé, Mariah Carey and Lady Gaga. Just another example of how different we both are. But then, Simone also wears a dress to school mufti days and I don't hold that against him.

Simone is only a useful double agent for a few weeks. Until he announces, "I'm not answering anymore questions about Leila Folger."

"Why not?"

“Because me and her are friends now. If you want more info – go ask her yourself.” His stern expression tells me he’s not kidding. “It’s obvious you have a thing for her. So be a man and talk to her.”

Me? With a ‘thing’ for #AngryGirl? Get real. She barely crosses my mind. Ever.

And when I see her name on the Hard Labor detention list, it’s curiosity and nothing more that makes me offer to switch supervision duties with Suvinia. Curiosity. And nothing more. That’s my story and I’m sticking to it…

4

It's the worst kind of day to be working outside. Sticky sweat and choking humidity. Barely a breeze anywhere. Leila is the only girl on Hard Labor. Along with a few junior students and Malua, who plays prop position on the rugby team.

"Hey Leila, hard labor? What have you been doing to deserve the worst SamCo has to offer?" A guy can be curious, can't he?

She scowls. Shrugs. "Nothing. Just a few too many late arrivals."

She's lying. The girl is a compulsive class-cutter. All the evidence is right there in front of me. "Really? It says here, you've been cutting class, umm PE class?" That's unexpected. "Why? I thought you were supposed to be Maleko's running nemesis?"

Of course she doesn't like my comment. This time I don't even get a glare. She just ignores me. Turns and stares at the distant coconut trees. Why do I even bother trying with this girl? I get to work. "Right people, let's get started so we can go home. Mr Raymond wanted the grass around the tennis courts cut."

The boys groan. I knew how they feel. Because of an inexplicable fascination with #AngryGirl, I am now stuck spending an afternoon in the hot sun supervising manual labor when I could be at home studying for tomorrows Physics test. Just great.

I try to hide my irritation when I tell her (nicely) to weed while we take on the long grass at the back of the court. By that point, I just want to get it over with. But instead of being grateful for getting the easy job, #AngryGirl is hostile.

"Excuse me? Why can't I cut grass too? Why should I do something different?"

Everybody stares at her. Disbelief. What is wrong with her? I explain that we use machetes to cut grass (not lawnmowers like you do back home…) That should have been enough for any regular sane palagi girl fresh from the civilized world. But not for her. Oh no.

"Yeah, so? Why can't I do that too?" With a hand on her hip and her chin stuck out defiantly, she reminds me of Simone when he's on the war path. "I know how to use a machete. I'm sure it's none of your concern anyway…"

I want to bite back at her. Especially since I was only trying to be helpful. And this is where it gets me? Hey, if that's how she wants to play it, then I'm not going to stand in her way. She's lying about using a machete. I know it. We all know it. She's going to look like a complete idiot and the thought gives me a perverse pleasure. Ha.

A smile. A grand gesture of supplication. "Hey, no problem. You want to cut grass with them, you go right ahead. I'm just here to supervise and make sure you serve your detention, that's all."

She grabs a machete from the pile. The others are just as excited as I am about seeing what she's going to do with it. Me and Malua exchange a look. One that says exactly what we think of knowitall *fiapoto* girls from America who have more attitude than common sense. She stands there for a few minutes studying that machete like its rocket science. We get tired of waiting and I motion for the others to get started. They spread out and the job begins.

#AngryGirl picks out a spot and swings too low. The flinty grating sound has her jumping. And the rest of us laughing. But quietly. Because we're trying to be gentlemen. Trying not to be rude. (And failing at it.) She huffs a deep breath and tries again. This time she swings too high and the blade slips along the top of the grass and narrowly misses her leg. She swears loudly. I feel bad now. This is going too far. The next attempt will probably see her hack into her calf and then I'll be stuck with First Aid duty in a school without a proper First Aid kit.

I stop her before she can get any worse. "Hey, you're going to hurt yourself there. Why don't you let me show you how to do it?"

She gives me a frozen look of polite fury. "I said I didn't need any help and I meant it. Thank you but I'm fine."

She's not fine. A spike of guilt nags at me. Because she's a lone girl in a gang of strange boys, taking on her first Hard Labor punishment in a new school and we had kind of egged her on by making fun of her. A sudden flash of my grandmother's disapproving face in my mind has me sighing. Mama wouldn't approve of this whole situation. Time to try being nice again. I soften my tone. Cut down on the mocking. "No come on, at least allow me to show you how to hold the blade properly. Just a little help before you chop your leg off. Or somebody else's."

She still isn't going to bend. I can see the inner struggle she's having. And then Malua settles it with his gruff, Godfather voice. "Don't be such a fiapoto girl. He's right. You don't know what you're doing. Listen to him." Malua doesn't speak much. And when he does, most people listen.

#AngryGirl glares. "Alright fine. Go ahead. Show me." Like she's doing me a massive favour by allowing me to give her a lesson. I'm tempted again to leave her. Call all the boys and walk away. Leave her there to be a bitch all by herself. But I squash that moment of meanness and instead give her quick instructions. How to hold the blade. How to swing it. How to lean. How to pull back. Then I move to cut the tall green swathes in front of us, several swings, a close up demo. But when I stop to give her the blade, I realize she wasn't even watching my demo. Instead she was staring away into the trees. Like she's bored out of her mind and has far better things to do with her time. Then waste it here with us.

I don't even try to keep the irritation from my voice. "You're supposed to be watching so you can figure out how to do this, now come here. Your turn. You try."

We watch as she takes the blade and moves to start cutting. She's still not holding the machete correctly. "Wait, not like that. Like this."

I don't get mad easily. But Leila is the exception. Because I'm getting mad. Real mad. I step in close so I can model how she should stand with it. "Bend your knees slightly, lean forward a bit and let your body follow the swing of the blade…"

And then it happens. I'm standing behind her. Pressed in close. We touch. I close my hand around her fingers on the machete handle. The length of my arm follows hers. Skin to skin. And it's like a jolt of electricity. I'm plugged into a live wire. From far away I hear myself reciting instructions of what to do with the machete but my every nerve end is lit up. This close to her, the very air tastes of something sweet that I can't put a name to. This close to her, the thick braid of hair swings and catches against my arm, revealing that spot at the back of her neck where strands of hair cling to her skin with the heat of the day. I can't stop staring down at her. I want to lean in even closer. I want to ask her what is that perfume? I want to feel her, know her, walk with her, laugh with her. All these things rush through me in a nanosecond. It must have only been a minute at the most that I was holding her hand, showing her what to do – but it's the longest minute of my life. It's a heat-filled, earth-shattering minute that's doing crazy things to me. It's a minute that drowns me.

She must know there's something wrong with me because she pulls away abruptly. "I got it, I got it."

A burn of shame fills me. She probably thinks I was sleazing onto her. What if she figures out what I was thinking? What I was feeling? I move several feet away and stand at a safe distance while she tries cutting grass again. I'm grateful everyone's eyes are on her and not me. Because there's stuff going on with me that I hadn't predicted. And that I'm wishing desperately would go away. And fast. Before anyone notices.

I have to do something. Fast. Burn it off, shut it down. *Think of something else Daniel. Horrible stuff. Do something. Anything! Stop it, make it go away.* I grab a machete. For an hour I concentrate on attacking grass, working furiously to get myself back under control.

By the time the detention is over, I'm good. Back on top. Ready to joke, smile, laugh. I dismiss the group and we all head to the water fountain with relief. I strip my shirt off and get wet. I hadn't planned on a sun workout today but now that it's done, my muscles feel good. The boys make the most of the water and again I feel sorry for the only girl amidst us. Left out. "So I bet you're glad that's over." I shake my hair and drops scatter. "Oops sorry."

She almost smiles. "That's alright, thanks. For your help today. I probably owe you my still intact leg."

It's such a welcome relief not to have her angry. She doesn't know what I was thinking and what I was feeling earlier. I'm safe. I laugh. "Actually all the boys are relieved they still have their legs to walk home on too, they were a bit worried when you started swinging that thing around."

Malua joins in. "Ay Daniel, I thought this girl was going to cut us all in pieces. Should never let a girl loose with a bush knife, ay?"

And just like that, Leila shuts down. #AngryGirl is back. "I don't know why you thought I wouldn't be able to handle it. I may not have ever used a machete before but there's no reason why I couldn't figure it out if given the opportunity. There's no reason to be such sexist jerks."

Stab, stab. This girl is unbelievable.

Malua whistles. "Sole man, Daniel. I don't think she likes our jokes."

She's bolting to leave us behind but I'm not letting her get away that easy. I grab at her arm. "What is with you? We're just kidding, don't you ever relax and just chill? You don't even know me!"

She shakes me off. "No, I don't know you. And you can be sure that I have no desire to."

She leaves. I want to smash things. I want to break something. Someone. Anyone. I go home. But instead of hitting the books like I should, I go to the back of the workshop. My makeshift gym. The one my grandfather helped me to put together. I strip down to shorts again and beat the crap out of the bag. I'm mad. At her. At myself for caring.

I don't get it. How can a girl go from giving you a hard-on to making you so mad you want to kill someone?

5

There's some things I keep to myself. Like the fact that for most of my life, I've had a thing about the ocean. I wouldn't go so far as to call it a phobia. But yeah, me and oceans, rivers, and swimming pools? We don't connect. My mother died in the ocean. Probable suicide. That may have something to do with it. Mama had always been open with me about her. That she had drowned right after I was born. That they had loved me as their own ever since.

So if water is not my thing – then why am I here again? It's two in the morning and I'm walking through the bush towards the freshwater pool that I know is out there, slapping at mosquitoes, grateful for the full moon so I don't trip over and end up face first in the dirt.

I've been having trouble sleeping. A couple of nights a week, it's the same thing. I wake up some time after midnight. Restless. Gotta get out of the house. I try working out on the old weights at the back of the workshop. Hoping to tire myself out so I can go back to sleep. No luck. Get in the truck and go for a drive. And every time, I end up here. At the pool at the back of Faatoia village. Where I get wet, swim for a bit, feel settled, and then go home. Then and only then will I get a good sleep.

So yeah, it makes no sense, but I'm here again. I can hear the waterfall before I get there. It gives me that uneasy feeling. I don't like it. But I still want it. *Ah, what the hell, let's get this over with.* The sooner I get wet, the sooner I can go home and go to sleep.

I break out of the tangled trees and stop short. Because there's someone else here.
It's a girl. She's standing in the black water with her back to me. She's tall, with long thick hair to her waist. But that's not enough to hide the fact that she's not wearing much. A black bikini thing. Which is a little unusual for Samoa. I'm caught off guard, so I just stand there for a minute and stare. She looks oddly familiar but I don't know why. I'm sure I don't know any girls who go swimming in the middle of the night. And while I stare at her, she raises her hands up to the sky and throws her head back. Silver moonlight ripples on bare, wet skin. The night suddenly gets very hot for me, very fast. Like a rush of music that hits you with emotion. A raw, ragged Eminem song about a sorceress and space-bound rocket ships.

You take my breath away...

And then I feel like a creepy stalker. Which makes me mad. This is my 2am hangout. What's this girl doing here?

I move closer. "What are you doing here?" I didn't mean it to sound as harsh as it did.

The girl is startled. She jumps, slips and falls. Goes under. Splashes wildly. The water isn't very deep so I wait for her to get back up. She doesn't. She keeps flailing all over the place. I feel bad now. She's probably freaked out big-time. I *am* a creepy stalker. And now she's going to drown in a foot of water because of me.

I go quick to the pool, grab her arm. It makes things worse. She pushes at my hand. Yells. "Get off me! I said get off. I know kung fu – I mean karate. And I have a weapon. I do. Get away!"

What the hell? She blindly hits out at me and falls over again. Goes under. She's like a drowning puppy now. Wildly kicking and hitting out at everything and nothing. Now I'm getting worried. Maybe she can't swim. Maybe she's scared of the water. Which makes no sense then that she would be out here all by herself. *Half-naked.* I'm trying to ignore the part of my brain that just said that. *Do something Daniel.*

I reach down and grab her firm enough that she can't shake me loose. Her skin is hot to the touch. Hot enough that I almost let her go. *That's weird.* I ignore the burn and drag her over to the side of the pool. Put her down on the ground. She turns over immediately, trying to get all that hair out of her face, wiping at her eyes, coughing and spluttering. I look at her and in that moment, I realize, *hey, I know you!* It's Leila. Very wet. Very flustered. And very half-naked. *Stop saying that. Stop noticing that.*

In that moment I'm happy it's her and not some total stranger, which would be *really* awkward. *Get honest.* Okay, I'm just glad because it's her. She's here. Right now. With me. I don't know how or why, but here she is. And I haven't drowned her. So yeah, I'm happy. I'm not sure why though, because the girl has been nothing but a mega-bitch to me from day one. Still, I laugh. "So which is it? Karate or kung-fu? Either way, I'm reeeally scared."

She glares up at me. Angry face. Angry eyes. The usual Leila. But the impact is kinda reduced because of her outfit. Or lack of it. Dammit, it's not even a real swimsuit. She'd been swimming in her underwear and that shit aint made for getting wet. I try not to let my eyes linger on how the material is outlining all kinds of stuff . But it's hard. In more ways than one. *Quick, think of something else. Say something. Do something.* Humor. I seize on it with relief - before she can accuse me of being a psycho stalker who can't take his eyes off her chest, blatantly outlined in thin, wet cotton.

I look down at her hostile self and shake my head, "And so this weapon of yours? Just where exactly would you be concealing that?"

But as usual with this girl, my joke misfires. Instead of laughing with me, she scrambles to her feet, grabbing at a towel that lies nearby. Once tightly wrapped in it, she hits me with a rush of rage. "What the hell do you think you're doing? Creeping around in the dark, sneaking up on people like that and then scaring them? And how dare you put your hands on me." She searches wildly for words. "You – you- you horrible creep!"

It cuts to hear her accuse me of what I'd kinda been worried about myself. Guilt makes me snap. Again. "Excuse me? Oh I get it, we're going for a three count – racist, sexist and now I'm potential rapist. Is there nothing you won't accuse me of?"

She stares back at me with her arms wrapped tightly around her chest, hanging on to that towel like she thinks I'm going to rip it off her. Chin raised defiantly. Moonlight trying its best to soften that angry face. Strands of wet hair. *What would she do if I kissed her?* Where in hell did that come from?

I forge ahead, trying to shut that voice up inside my head. "Last time I checked, this pool didn't belong to you. I have every right to come swimming here. And when a clumsy female falls over in the water and looks like she's drowning in only two feet of water – it's considered gentlemanly behaviour to pull her out. In fact, most girls would then say *thank you* for helping them." I put as much ice as I can into my voice. To cover up the heat that's inside me.

For a moment she looks hurt. "Oh…" But it's fleeting as she launches back into offensive mode. "You shouldn't have scared me like that. That wasn't nice. It's the middle of the night, out here in the middle of nowhere, so of course I was gonna think you were attacking me or something."

A sudden image hits me. Of some guy chancing upon her tonight. Some other guy besides me. Some guy who would have jumped at the opportunity to do exactly that. Attack her. Hurt her. That makes me mad. I tense all over, trying not to clench my fists as I think of what I would do to that faceless guy who tried it. What's wrong with me?! Everything about this girl has me twisted in a gut-wrenching tangle of feelings that I can't decipher. I don't like it. Why in hell do I care what happens to her anyway?

I try to sound casual. "I don't know what you were thinking being out here alone anyway. Are you crazy? Yes, this is Samoa and we don't have the same number of psycho killers running around like you do back in the States but still, it's just stupid for a girl to be out swimming in her underwear by herself. What were you thinking?"

A shadow of doubt flickers across her face, "I know, I mean – I didn't think anybody would be out here so late. And I've come here a few times now and never seen anyone. And I didn't think I was trespassing, so I didn't know it would cause any trouble and back home you woudn't catch me out by myself in a forest in a million years…"

She's babbling now. Stumbling over her words. Wet, bedraggled, kinda cold in the cool wet night. For the first time, I see a different Leila. Not mad. Not hostile. Not reactionary. Just sad. That's what it is. This girl is hurting. And that cuts me. *I want to hold you. Wrap you in my arms and hold you close. Safe.* Again, I'm messed up. A mental shake. *What the hell is wrong with you man?*

She comes to a shaky halt, "Oh why am I telling you anything?" She turns her back on me and takes a deep breath. I can see the bone outline of her shoulder blades in the moonlight. Thin. Frail. *Is she shaking? Is she crying? Oh shit.* My grandfather always told me that a man should honor and respect women "and whatever you do, don't make them cry. Never hurt a woman, you hear me son? They bear burdens that we men can never hope to understand. We are nothing without them. Never hurt a woman." I think of his stern words as I watch this girl try to hide her tears from me and I feel like shit. I've messed up. I've hurt her and I don't even know how.

"Hey, look, I'm sorry okay? I come here a lot and I was kinda surprised to find anybody else here. I didn't mean to scare you." I try to speak soft and low. She's trembling on the edge of a cliff and I'm freaking out big-time that she's going to lose it completely.

Again, she takes me off guard because she gives me a huge plastic smile. A smile so forced that it's scary. "Oh, don't even worry about it. I over-reacted. It happens. Look, I'll get out of your way. Thanks for your help in the water. Have a nice swim." She grabs her clothes and starts backing away, smiling that same bright smile. I don't want her to go. I want her to stay. When else, where else will I get this chance to talk to her – when she's not in full attack mode? There had been a sliver of a connection, a silken thread linking us and now she's going to leave. I want to ask her to stay. But instead I stand there and watch her back away from me.

She trips over something in the bushes behind her, falls down and lands on her butt. Hard. "Owww!"

The look on her face is classic. Startled. Aggrieved. I'm about to smile and move to help her up but again this girl does the unexpected. She bursts into tears. Just like that. She buries her face in her hands, her shoulders shake and her whole body cries. I don't think. I just act. I do what I've been wanting to do for the last half hour. I don't stop to think what she will say or how she will react. I kneel beside her and take her in my arms.
"Hey, it's okay. You're gonna to be okay." I want it to be true. Only I don't know how to make it so.

I hold her. Wet, trembling, crying. And it feels like coming home. This girl is a stranger but there's nothing strange or unfamiliar about her body against mine. Something deep inside me knows her. I don't know how or why. But Leila in my arms is the most familiar, most welcoming thing. Like a piece of me had been missing and I never knew it.

If I were blind, I would know you by the lick of you, the feel of you. The something sweet and wet of you.

I want to get her out of the mud. I flex, lift her off the ground and walk to the rocky poolside. Her head on my shoulder, her face turned into my chest under a fall of wet hair. I hate to let her go but the mere touch of her sears me. So I place her on smooth rocks and sit beside her just keeping my shoulder in contact with hers. And then, I just let her cry.

'*Hurt is a spring that needs to flow freely Daniel. If you lock it up inside you, if you build a dam to contain it, that hurt builds up and poisons you.*' Mama told me when Papa died. And so we had cried together. And alone. And she was right. Because after a while, the hurt wasn't a rushing torrent anymore that threatened to drown you. Instead it was a gentle ache, a constant reminder of the one you loved who was no longer with you. It still hurt but not in a hurtful way that ripped you to pieces.

I remember Mama's advice and so, here, now, with Leila - I don't speak. I don't shush her or soothe her. I just sit there and let this angry girl cry. And me and the forested night feel her pain. When she's done, her face tells me how embarrassed she is about having me see her at her low, vulnerable moment. She's a mess. Face sticky with tears and flushed red, Puffy eyes and snotty nose. I get her T-shirt and give it to her with what I hope is an encouraging smile. The last thing I want is for her to find a reason to blast me again. "Sorry, I didn't come equipped to comfort a damsel in distress."

She wipes her face before looking up at me. She's still a mess but now she's calmer. It's like she's cried out all pieces of that angry girl who hates everybody and everything. Leaving behind just Leila. A girl who is ready to sit at ease with me and look into my eyes. It hits me then how close we actually are. I can feel her breath against my face. See the flush of each eyelash on her cheek. If I move just the slightest few inches, lean forward, my lips will graze her forehead. I'm not sure why that thought even occurs to me. I brush away wet strands of hair stuck to her face and her skin is hot on my fingers. I don't want to stop touching her. I have to force myself to let go.

She breaks the silence with an apology. "You must think I'm such an idiot, crying like that. Whew, I'm sorry."

"Sorry for what?"

"I didn't mean to fall apart like that. Thanks for being so cool about it."

I like her falling apart. It means that she turns into this nice person who doesn't have any energy left for hating me. Yelling at me. Yeah, if I could have my way, this girl would fall apart every time I see her. So I could have this again. Right here, right now. No walls, No barriers. No misunderstandings. But then that's probably not something a guy should say to a girl. "Hey, don't worry about it. I've been there. Why do you think this is one of my favourite places to come to?" I lie. Yeah, so I lie. The great, wonderful Daniel stretches the truth sometimes. But I want her to feel comfortable about hanging out in midnight pools and crying in forests.

I can't stop staring at her. And now she's a thousand miles away. You can tell. Drowning in a sadness so huge that it leaches out of her every pore. It's in her eyes, in her breathing, on her skin – everywhere. She's beside me – but she isn't.

"Where were you just now?"

"Nowhere. I mean here. Right here. With you." She's hesitating. I want to know what sadness imprisons her? I want to know it. See it. Feel it. Access it. I want it more than anything else.

"You were not. You were a thousand miles away." I try to tease it out of her, knowing that her stubbornness can kick in any minute and slam a door on this unexpected closeness. "Come on, you can't possibly think of keeping any secrets from me now."

She laughs. She actually laughs! The meanest girl I've ever met laughs. And it's real. And light. Finally, after all the times I've tried to get this girl to be happy with me. She laughs. And it's a beautiful sound.

I want to spend my life making you laugh… WTF did that come from?!

There is nothing but laughter in her voice. "Okay, you're right. I mean, what could the girl who has weapons galore concealed in her underwear possibly have to hide from you?"

Now I knew we're getting somewhere. She's cracked a joke! I laugh along with her. Relieved big-time. "You're right, I don't know if I'm brave enough to find out."

She pokes her tongue at me. A quick, unexpected gesture that wrinkles her nose. She's cute, playful even. Words I would never have used to describe her. I try not to focus on her tongue. Her lips. The way her eyes light up when she smiles. But as quickly as it comes, it's gone. The sadness is back. That distant lost emptiness in her eyes. Can't she ever just stay in one emotion zone?

"See there. You're doing it again. You're miles away. Something has got you wrapped up so tight it won't let you go. What is it?" I'm not going to let this go. Whatever it takes, I'm going to get it out of her.

"Alright, I was thinking of my Dad. He died. Eight months ago…" The truth is a hit to the midsection. Whatever I'd been expecting, it isn't this. She goes on, telling me about her father. It hurts. I can see it in every piece of her. I hurt with her and for her. Remembering Papa and how sick he'd been. The long, painful process of dying. But she had lost her Dad suddenly. Abruptly. It's ripping her up to even talk about it. She stumbles mid-sentence. It seems right to put my arm around her shoulders.

"Hey. I'm here. Breathe. There you go. Just breathe."
For a moment her body stiffens in mine. She's debating whether to shove me away. And then the decision is made. She releases a taut breath. Relaxes. Looks into my eyes. And then away, dropping her gaze from mine. This girl doesn't like closeness. Doesn't like it when someone invades her personal space. I should just move away. But I don't want to. Against my better judgement, I raise her face up so she can't hide anymore. "Are you okay? I'm sorry I made you talk about it. I didn't mean to upset you."

She shakes her head, "I'm okay. I haven't talked about it to anyone. It's hard. But I want to talk about him as well too, even though it hurts so bad you know what I mean?"

Did I ever. It feels good to find common ground. A link. Connection that maybe her psycho anger can't break. "Yes I do."

I can tell by the look on her face that she doesn't believe me. So I have to explain. Show a bit more of myself than I would like to. Maybe it's the whole *sitting in the moonlight* thing. Doing funny things to my brain. Making it alright to tell this strange girl, personal stuff I wouldn't tell anyone else. "My mother died when I was very young. I never knew her really, so it's different for me. Talking to family about her makes her come alive for me somehow but still it's tough because it reminds me how much I miss having her."

It's the right move. She grabs at my words like they're ice water in this sauna-heat. "Exactly. Nobody loves my dad the way I do, nobody loved me the way he did…"

She's giving me more pieces of herself. Jealously guarded fragments of brokenness. "How about your mom? Can't you talk to her about it?"

She shakes her head, scrunches her face up. "My mother died when I was a baby. I never knew her. That's one reason I came to Samoa. So I could get to know her family and maybe know her. Some stupid idea that's turned out to be."

Her disappointment is thick and heavy. I feel guilty. Which is dumb because it's not like it's my fault personally that she's not having a good time in Samoa. "So Samoa isn't exactly turning out to be what you planned. And your family here? Who are they?"

What's her story. How did she end up here on the other side of the world? What is she being punished for?

"My aunty Matile and uncle Tuala – they're the Sinapati family. We live just round the corner from the stadium, Apia Park."

That doesn't tell me much. How to get more info out of her? I couldn't very well hit her with 'why did your palagi family send you to live with us coconuts?' No. That wouldn't go down very well. "So do you have lots of random cousins living with you? Our extended family living must be kind of a shock for a spoilt only child like you."

"Hey, watch it, I can still take you on, you know. Spoilt only children are infamous for their tempers. Actually they don't have children of their own and nobody stays with them but me. There's always cousins coming over though from next door, round about meal time. Aunty Matile is a major grouch but she's an amazing cook. Especially when you're used to living on fast food. Me and Dad, we weren't much for cooking. But we had the Chinese takeout number on speed dial." She laughs and I laugh with her. But inside I feel sorry for her.

In those few sentences I get a picture painted for me of this girl's life. Before. With Solo Dad. The two of them, a tag team against the world. Sitting in an empty house. Eating takeaway every night. It's bleak. But she's a girl who would hate it if you showed pity for her. So I keep it light. "Glad to hear that at least the food is to your liking. And how are you finding SamCo?"

We talk. For what seems like an hour or so. Yeah, it's unexpected. Me. #AngryGirl. Sitting in a forest. Talking. Laughing. And when we're done. When she finally leaves - I can't stop the goofy grin on my face. Hi-fiving the awesomeness that is quite possibly – the best night of my life.

6

It's an important game. Samoa College facing off against Leififi College on their home ground. It's our second time playing them this year. First time had been an uneasy draw. Cocky bastards hadn't stopped talking about it ever since. They are out to make history and win the championship. We weren't about to let that happen. My last year as captain of the First XV? I am not going to let it happen. There's a lot riding on this game. So why did I ask Leila to come? I don't need that extra pressure.

It's a good game though. Intense. Physical. Three people have to be carried off the field. I score four tries. *Did she see me? Was she looking?* Knowing she's there makes it different. Has me on edge. I run faster. Stand taller. Hit harder. Push more, push it to the edge more. Throwing myself over the try line feels even better knowing she's somewhere in the crowd. I'm on a natural high. A rush. We win. And it feels good. The boys go wild celebrating the win, Maleko leads them in an impromptu Gangnam style celebration dance.

Laughing. Pushing. Group hug. I turn away from it all to look for her. Why do I keep feeling the need to see her? Know where she is? I see others in Samoa College orange and yellow, but I can't make out Leila. Where is she?

I'm looking for her, so I miss it initially, when a couple of our team get into a scuffle with some Leififi boys. Sore losers know how to ruin a good buzz. The shouting brings me back to the moment. Two boys are at each other's throats. Teachers too far away to do anything. I move fast. Go to break it up. Easy to do when you're taller than the rest of the crowd. Everybody's getting excited. Upping the adrenaline. Shouts. Pushing. Shoving. A whole lot of wannabe-bad-asses.

"Quit it. Break it up." I pull our boy out of it first, push him behind me so I can snap at the Leififi uniform who is still trying to spit out the usual tough talk. "Yeah, whatever. Get back over there, fool."

I should have kept my guard up. Should have been more alert. *Stupid, Daniel.* I'm pulling our boy back through the crowd with my mind still on Leila. Hoping she doesn't leave before I get a chance to talk to her. Then something hits me. A bottle. Luckily the idiot who attacked me must be a whole lot shorter because his blow catches me on the side of my head. It still hurts though. A lot. The glass shatters. Blood gushes. I'm dazed. And then I'm mad. I look around. Anger surges. Crashes on an immovable reef. I say some things that would have Mama washing my mouth out with soap for. I take down the first Leififi uniform I can reach. I can't see properly because of the blood-edged rage that clouds my vision. It doesn't matter. You don't need to see what you're hitting for it to hurt. My fists connect. Again and again.

Everything goes crazy. People are beating up on each other all around me. Yelling. I stand up. I can't see past the raging crowd around me. And that's when the rage leaves. Because all I can think of is her.

Leila. Where is she?

Shame. Sour and bitter. What was I doing? Beating up some pathetic loser when I should have been making sure she was alright. I asked her to this game. And now it had turned into a full-on brawl. So this is what wild panic feels like. I shove people aside. Searching. I call out her name, trying to make myself heard over the madness around me. I catch sight of a cluster of SamCo girls standing far back from the mayhem. Over by the trees that line the road. Relief floods me. So strong it's dizzying. *Get a grip man*. What is wrong with me? I turn back to face the crowd. Steel myself. I'm the Captain. The Head Boy prefect. This is my responsibility. I pick out Malua and head for him first. He's standing immovable in the midst of scuffling boys, smashing someone with a well-placed fist every now and again if they do anything stupid. Like step on his toes. Or wander into his airspace.

"Malua, I need your help. We have to break this up."

He doesn't say anything. Just nods. Then he walks into the nearest knot of fighters and easily sweeps them apart. Carving a path effortlessly. I have to smile. I would never want Malua on any other team but mine. I leave him to it and move on to separate Maleko from his adversary. "That's enough. Stop it. Now!"

Both boys breathe heavily and swear a lot. At me and each other. But they stop. "Good. Now help me get this mess cleaned up."

I turn to target another cluster of boys when I see her. The flash of orange and yellow. The thick braids. She's pushing her way through the crowd. Her height makes her stand out. It also makes her an easy target. She's only a few feet away from me, but in that riot, it may as well have been an ocean.

"Leila!" I shout her name. Just as a Leififi student leans in to confront her. And then I lose sight of her as a tangled knot of rugby players bang into me and together we all go down in a heap. On the ground, it's a panicked few minutes to wrestle people off me. *Out of my way*! I claw my way up. Uncaring now of who I hit. Who I shove out of my way. I can't see her. Where is she? "Leila!"

There she is! Everything moves in slow motion. Like in a bad horror movie. I see it happen and I can't move. Can't reach her. Can't do anything to stop it. The boy in the beige and navy uniform has his back to me. I can see her face. Eyes wide. Fear. So much fear that it chokes me. Her fear. I can see it. Taste it. Feel it.

I shout "No!" and even as I force the word out, the Leififi boy hits her across the face. A blow to the cheek. It stings. I flinch at the impact, at the pain/hurt that isn't mine.

I fight my way closer. There's too many people in front of Leila now. Can't see her clearly. And it's killing me. I'm drowning in a blue haze of rage. There's a distant roaring in my ears like a faraway ocean. And then I'm through. Just in time to see her attacker fall back away from her. He stumbles, hands to his face, screaming in agony. I'm going to go after him and strangle him with my bare hands but the look on her face stops me. She stands there in the center of the madness with shock, outrage on her face. And a massive red welt on her cheek. She holds her hands out, studying them with horror. Like they're blood covered or something. She's oblivious to the pushing and shoving around her. She must be in shock. If I don't get her away from there, someone else will hurt her. I reach her. Bend in close to her ear. "Leila, are you alright?"

She doesn't answer. Just gives me and her hands that same horror-stricken look. I try to shield her from the ruckus around us. Wishing I could snap my fingers and get her out of here in a heartbeat. Muttering to myself, "Where did that guy go? Where is he?" I've never wanted to hurt someone so bad. I can't see him. He's lost in the crowd. And Leila is still standing there with her feet rooted to the spot. Not crying. Not shaking. Not speaking. Just with that same stunned expression on her face.

I take her hand. It feels right in mine. "Come on, let's get you out of here." She doesn't resist. Just allows me to take her with me. Through the crowd. Across the field. To my truck in the parking lot. Have to get her away. Have to keep her safe.

Beside the truck, I turn her to face me. She's pliant in my arms, like a rag doll. Bewildered eyes cut me. A thousand knives of guilt. Red stains her cheek. Bruised capillaries swollen with impact. This is my fault. I did this to her. I let this happen. "I'll kill him. I'll find him and I'll kill him." Rage and shame power my fist as it slams into the truck. The pain is nothing compared to the guilt cutting me up inside.

I wait for her to yell at me. Curse. Storm away. Hate me. Instead her voice is soft. "Daniel, please don't be angry. I'm alright. Honest."

I would feel better if she was classic #AngryGirl and hit me with hostility. I deserve it. "I'm sorry. I'm not mad at you. I'm sorry I asked you to come to the game. And then didn't make sure you were alright. I'm so sorry." If I could have apologized a thousand times I would have. She should hate me. Instead she looks up at me with a bewildered tenderness in her eyes. Without my permission, my fingers go to touch her face, the red welt, her cut lip. Wishing I had magic hands that could heal. Wishing I could make it all disappear. In that moment, it hits me. I can't lie to myself anymore. This girl means something to me. Something powerful. Something that grips my chest tight and won't let go. Something that sucks the air from my lungs and makes time slow to a grinding halt. What is it?

And then she makes a face at me. "Eww, you smell awful. And you look worse. Never mind about me, what happened to you?"

Grateful to have the taut moment broken, I laugh. This is a Leila I can handle. One I can tease. Bicker with. "Don't try to spare my feelings or anything! Let me think, I've just played a rugby game, had a bottle smashed on my head, been punched at by a couple of sore losers and then almost lost my mind trying to get to you."

That last bit sneaks in when I'm not looking. Betraying me. I'm hoping she doesn't pick up on the faint desperation in those few words. Have to change the topic. Quick. So I go on the attack. "What were you doing there? …What were you thinking? I was sure you would have been safe with the other students by the road. You know, where it was *safe*." I want her to rage back at me. Be prickly unpleasant Leila so the status quo between us can be reasserted.

Instead she looks panicked. Stumbles over her words. Unsure. "I was confused about where to run. I got mixed up and then couldn't get out of there. And then that Leififi boy he got a little carried away with everything."

She's nervous. Afraid. Of me? This is even worse. She probably hates all rugby players now. She's never going to want to talk to me again. How am I going to make this right? "We need to get you some ice. Before that really starts to swell. You're going to look like one of David Tua's opponents after a fight." Oh yeah, that was smooth. Every girl's dream. To be compared to a heavy weight boxer. No wonder I don't have a girlfriend.

She flashes me a half-smile. Maybe that blow to her face affected her radar for detecting fools. "Thanks. What a comforting thought."

I take advantage of her momentary lapse in judgement. I know the police would have been called. I want her out of there before the situation goes up a level to DefCon three. I wrench open the truck door. "Come on. Get in. I'll give you a ride home."

I haven't had a girl ride in my truck since…okay, since NEVER. I shove the X-Men comic under the seat. I hope she doesn't notice the suspicious abundance of Snickers bar wrappers on the floor . Aww no, what if she gets welding grease on her clothes? *Stop it Daniel*. The girl just got her face slammed into someone's fist. Dirty clothes are last on her list of concerns right now. She gets in. The seat's kinda high and sitting there makes her skirt move up a little. I start the truck and try not to look at her legs next to me. I want to take her to the hospital to get her face checked out but she insists on going home, giving me vague directions.

When we get to the house, I watch while she walks up to the door and lets herself in. I wish I knew her well enough so I could follow her. Get her an ice pack or something. But I'm gutless. Plus, she's already told me there's nobody else home, so it wouldn't be right to go inside with her anyway. So instead I drive home, worrying about her all the way. Maleko texts me about the fight. Yeah, the police showed up but nobody had been seriously hurt. Just one Leififi kid had been taken away in a police car to the hospital. I'm not looking forward to the next day because I know there'll be hell to pay with the Principal. And as Head boy and team Captain, I'm going to have to do a lot of damage control.

That should be uppermost on my mind that night. But it isn't. When dinner's done, after helping Mama with the dishes and once alone in my room – I can't shake Leila from my thoughts. I get her Aunt's number from directory and call her house but a stern voice tells me that she's asleep.

Homework is a meaningless jumble. Sleep keeps running away from me. No way do I want to go back to the forest pool. Not tonight. Not without Leila. Music might help – it's always been my life-raft. A part of my soul. My bedroom walls are covered with lyrics and music sheets. Three years ago I took all my savings from my after-school job at the workshop and bought a sleek stereo-mixer system that takes up more space in my bedroom than my bed. Mama had frowned and warned me that while music was important, "schoolwork must always come first." I didn't argue with her. Then or now. She's right. Schoolwork does come first. But music isn't a choice. Or an option. It's like breathing. Essential. I get my guitar and let its song get me through jumbled thoughts, feelings. How to deal with the guilt? How to make sense of the feelings that churn inside me when it comes to Leila? I can't figure her out. In the last 72 hours she's shown me so many different pieces of herself and I still can't make them all fit together. I don't know who she really is, which pieces are real and which are only pieces of a shattered smokescreen.

I grab my phone. Turn to the one person who is guaranteed to be an expert on girls and their weird ways. Simone.

U up?

Simone - *4 u? Always. Up an redy.*

Haha. Funny.

Simone - *I try. Wat do u want?*

*I messed up. I invitd #AngryGirl 2 rugbygame. Massive fight aftr. She got caught in it. Some Leififi piece of sh** hit her in face.*

Simone - *WTF? Where were U? Why didn't u look out 4 her?!*

Thanx. I alredy feel like crap abt it.

Simone - *Is she alrite?*

I thnk so. Do u thnk I stil hav a chance?

Simone - *A chance 4 wat?*

To b friends. U knw, to have her NOT hate on me all the time.

Simone - *"Friends" watevr. U bettr thnk of something really nice 2 do 4 her 2moro.*

Any ideas?

Simone - *No. Do I look like a messed up American girl who's nevr pluckd her eyebrows 2 u? Take off yr shirt 4 her. Do a MagicMike. That mite work.*

Be serious.

Simone - *I am. She calls u Chunk Hunk. That's gotta mean something.*

She calls me wat?!

Simone - *Chunk Hunk. U r all muscle and no brains 2 her. She can't take her eyes off u most of time.*

Chunk Hunk sounds like peanut butter. I want 2 b more thn a bread spread 2 her.

Simone – *Ask her out somewhere. Quiet. Private. Giv her a chance 2 talk 2 u. Hang out. Bt keep yr physical distance. Impress her with yr intellect & humor. (If u hav any, LMAO)*

Ok. Thanx. I think.

Simone - *Anytime. I dnt knw why u stressing over her 4. I wd b so much less trouble.*

I knw. But u wd get bored with me & break my heart. I not exciting enuf pulili 4 u.

Simone - *2 true. Leave me alone nw. I need my beauty sleep.*

Simone's advice seems solid. But I'm still ripped with doubts. Questions. Not for the first time, I wish my grandfather was here. So I could ask him about Leila. Or at least about girls in general. I love Mama, I'm close to her but I don't want to ask her about this mess of emotions. About a girl. Papa had been my best friend. In all things. My rock. I'd never brought up specific girl trouble with him, but if he were alive, I know he would help me now.

Papa, what would you say? What would you suggest I do? What advice would you give me?

I miss him. And then I remember something. Papa had laughingly told me about seeing Mama for the first time. …

****

"She was a fierce woman, even then son." A quiet laugh as he shook his head. "Not easy to approach. I was new to the island, just moved there from Tafahi and starting my welding shop. Went to church and there she was. For a woman so short, she was a bit scary with her direct stare. Eyes like speckled brown cowry shell. She was a woman who saved her smiles in reserve. For people that really mattered. When we met, I only got a nod. A raised eyebrow. She had a reputation for being a healer. But not a warm, friendly one. I didn't understand the whisperings about her then. I only knew that many discouraged me from approaching her. People had great respect for her but not many knew her. I didn't care what people said though. She fascinated me right from the start."

"So what did you do? How did you end up together?" I prompted.

A smile and a wink. "She was a healer so I knew she wouldn't turn away an injured man. I had a little accident in the workshop and went to her for help."

I was surprised AND admiring, "Papa, you FAKED an injury for a girl!?"

Grandfather laughed, "No son. Even worse, I deliberately burnt my arm on a welder so I could get her attention. The whole time she was taking care of my burn, I kept cracking jokes, trying to make her smile. No luck. When she was done, I asked how I could pay for the treatment and she looked me right in the eyes and said, *You can pay me by not hurting yourself on purpose and wasting my time and my medicines.*"

"SNAP! Busted. So then what?"

"I apologized with flowers every day until she agreed to go out with me. I wore her down with persistence." The old man shook his head at the memories. "I wanted to take her somewhere special but Niuatoputapu is very small. I had to think of a way to make an ordinary place special. Make it magic. So I chose a spot in the inland bush, up in the hills. A spot where flowers grew and you could see the blue ocean. I made us a picnic lunch and then before I took her there, I blindfolded her so she didn't know where we were going. And when our time there was finished, I blindfolded her again. I told her, that way – she would never be able to find her way there again without me. That way, it would remain secret, special, magical in here." Papa tapped the side of his forehead. "And in here." He patted his chest softly with a faraway smile on his face. "Every year after our wedding, before we moved away from Niuatoputapu, I would blindfold her and take her back to our secret spot. I'm sure she eventually figured out where it was but it didn't matter. Forty years later my son, and she still makes every day magic for me."

I looked at my grandfather's weathered, lined face alight with a quiet kind of joy and I told myself – that's the kind of love I want. One day.

****

The memories have me smiling. It's like getting girl advice from beyond the grave. Hmm…if it worked for Papa, maybe it can work for me?

I jump up off the bed and put some U2 on. Glad because I have a plan. It's decided. I'm going to go with blindfolds, poetry, flowers and straight up conversation. Oh yeah, and ninja stars.

7

Everything changes when there's a girl involved. When there's feelings that weren't there before. A regular school day feels like game day. Tense. A buried edge of excitement. Wondering how the game will go. Body alive, alight in readiness. That's how it feels, going to school knowing Leila will be there. Knowing I'm going to see her. Talk to her. Ask her out.

When I finally see her, she's getting off a bus that's blaring the Venga Boys. She's wearing black sunglasses and she's not smiling. She doesn't look frightened or delicate or sad like she did yesterday. I almost wimp out and let her walk past me. But the memory of a lonely girl crying in my arms beside a midnight pool reminds me she has a softness inside that daggered edge of hostility. Reminds me we had – we *have* – a connection.

I call after her, "Leila, wait up!"

Half the bloody school turns around. Dammit. Gossip coconut wire ready to buzz. I ignore them and walk over to her. She smiles. It's only a very half-hearted smile but it's a smile, so I'm taking it. "I've been waiting for you. I wasn't sure if you'd come to school today. I called your house last night to check on you, but a lady said you were sleeping. How are you?" I check out the side of her face. "Hey, that doesn't look too bad, you heal fast."

She takes her time answering and I'm super conscious of the eyes on my back. Curious and fascinated. "I'm fine. I slept for hours yesterday when you dropped me off and I feel so much better this morning."

Now she looks like she's in a rush to get away. To get rid of me. But I'm determined not to be shaken off. *I wore her down with persistence...forty years later and she still makes every day magic for me son.* I take her bag and walk with her. "Are you sure? Here, let me carry your bag."

She can't very well take off. Not when I'm hanging on to her schoolbag. So she speeds up the pace, rushing us towards the assembly area. We walk together up the long drive. Maleko and the boys are on the field. They stop their game so they can watch us. It's Maleko's turn to laugh and grin and tease me from the side-lines. I hope Leila can't see him miming some grinding Dirty Dancing moves in our direction. But she's oblivious, still babbling away, reassuring me she's fine. And doesn't need my help. Now Maleko is air kissing an imaginary girl and moaning loudly, '*Oooh Daniel, don't stop!*' The rest of the team think he's hilarious and they're cheering him on. I'm gonna kill him...She's going to notice, any minute now...

Saved by the bell. "I gotta go, I'm doing the assembly today. I'll see you later?" I almost throw her bag at her, I'm so desperate to leave so I can go shut Maleko up. Almost forget the ninja star I made for her with the U2 lyrics inside. Turn back. "Just something I made for you. Catch you later."

The rest of the morning I feel slightly sick. Thinking about her opening my note. Reading it. Hoping I haven't made a huge mistake. I don't see her again until after lunch. She's in an empty corridor, on her hands and knees picking up scattered books and papers. So relieved to find her alone. Good. So nobody can witness my crash and burn if she tells me to get lost. *Keep it light Daniel.* "Hey, there you are. I've been looking for you. Want to ask you something."

She stands up and gives me the evil glare. Aww shit. "Ask me what?"

It's too late to back out now. Have to keep going. Trying to find some words. "If you read my note…and if…if you're doing anything today after school?"

I've caught her by surprise. And surprise makes her talk too much. What is it with girls and their abundance of words? "Oh. No. I mean yes. I mean – no, I'm not doing anything after school. And I mean yes, I did read your note. Thanks. I…uh…it's not what I expected."

Uh oh. Is that a good or bad thing? "What do you mean? What did you expect?"

"Nothing. I just didn't expect anybody here to listen to U2. It's not the usual choice of music for the usual 21st century teenager."

That doesn't sound bad. I think. "I guess I'm not your usual 21st century teenager then." Smile. Smile. Smile so she doesn't see how nerves are tearing you up. Aaargh, this is worse than getting stuck in a scrum. I should have listened to Simone... '*Do a Magic Mike. Take your shirt off.*' Remembering that makes smiling a whole lot easier.

"No, I guess not." She's smiling. This is going good. It's working! But then she turns and starts walking away. *WTH?!*

"Hey, where are you going? You didn't let me finish."

She stops. Looks back at me. "Oh. Sorry. Did you want something?"

Yes, I want you to stop turning my head and my heart inside out. I want you to please, for once, be an open book… "Yeah. I wanted to make it up to you. For yesterday. For what was probably the worst day of your school life. I thought maybe we could go somewhere. Do something. Give me a chance to show you a better side of Samoa? Umm, of me?" I sound like an idiot. Idiot. Idiot. Idiot!

She's not saying anything. Just staring up at me. Forget it. This was a dumb idea. "Hey, if you don't want to, that's okay. I get it. You didn't exactly have an amazing first time out with me. I mean, asking you to come to a rugby game that turns into a brawl where you get beat up is not really an ideal way to impress a girl is it?" Smile. Act like you don't care. Smile.

"No – I mean yes. I want to. Sure. We can hang out. Today. I'll do it. No problem. I don't mind." She gives in with a semi-sour shrug. But she didn't say *no, get lost.* That's something, right?

"Great. I'm parked at the back by the tennis courts. I'll meet you there after school. You remember the green bomb right?"

I take off for class. On a high. I did it. I asked her out. And she said yes. If she was mad about getting slammed at the game, then she wouldn't have agreed to hang out, right?

****

The afternoon together went better than I hoped it would. The blindfold thing freaked her out a little and for a moment, I could tell she was debating whether or not to agree to it. But later, when I explained it to her, there was a light in her eyes, her voice, her face - telling me she liked it. She liked it a lot. *Thanks Papa.*

At the mountain stream, she dropped her guard enough so we did nothing but talk. Laugh. And talk some more. It was easy. Comfortable. It felt right. Like I'd known her all my life. I was trying to ignore the voice in my head that added - '*And you want to keep knowing her for the rest of your life.*' Because it was way too soon to be feeling this way about a person. Like you can't imagine laughing or living without her.

The whole afternoon out with Leila surprised me. She was funny. Sarcastic. A little bit twisted. She also had no clue how girls usually talked or behaved. I thought back to conversations with Mele. Last year before Papa died. When everybody and their dog had been telling me how much the girl wanted me. What a great couple we would make. How perfect we would be together. She had thought so too. I know her parents liked the idea. Her Dad was our rugby coach. And her mum was a hard-core supporter, driving people to all the games to cheer us, bringing after-game refreshments for us. The problem was that I liked Mele's parents a whole lot more than I liked her. Yeah, she was pretty. And yeah I did try to hang out with her. For a while. We even went together to the Rugby Awards Social. But Mele was so sure of herself that it scared me. We would eat lunch together and she liked to sit and rip everyone to shreds, critiquing everything from their hair to the way they walked. Or talked. It got old fast. I started inventing excuses not to hang out with her. And then Papa got sick and all the unimportant stuff in my life got shelved.

Including Mele.

When I started back at school this year, she was with Maleko. And that suited me just fine. Sure it was a little annoying to have your best friend's girlfriend be a girl that you had sort of been hanging out with a lot. But only because it meant she went everywhere that Maleko did. And then I had to see her. And be nice to her. Even when I was bored out of my mind. Maleko was a player so I looked forward to the day when he would find someone else to catch his eye. Mele was coldly calculating so until she found someone else with more status then the Vice Captain of the rugby team – she was staying put. It meant me and Maleko didn't hang out as much as we used to. Which was okay too. Because I had work deadlines chasing me 24-7.

I couldn't imagine two girls more different from each other. Where Leila was rude and obnoxious to your face – Mele had perfected the art of laughing and smiling at people so they never had a clue she was hating on them behind their backs. Where Leila slouched and stumbled around the place with her hair in those thick braid things – Mele glided. Graceful. Bestowed regal smiles all around her. Like she was a Miss Samoa beauty queen.

Nobody could call Leila a beacon of sunshine or anything. But when she did smile at you? Or laugh with you? It was like the rush of surf on the beach. Hit, crash the air out of you, bubble and foam. Tumble you. Then before you even have time to catch your breath and get your bearings – it pulls back. Disappears. Leaving you knocked out and gasping for breath, trying to stand. Wondering, what in hell happened?

The afternoon with Leila ranks right up there on my list of All-Time Favorite Things. I can't wait to see her again.

8

I'm on my way to P.E, running late, when there's a commotion in the corridor. A traffic jam. I push through hoping it's not a fight. I'm not in the mood to break up a bust-up.

But it's not a fight. Or even an argument. It's Leila. She's standing there in a sea of confused faces, reeling. Swaying like she's drunk. Hands over her face she screams, "Help me." WTH?

Someone laughs. Someone else mutters, 'Pe valea ea! Is she crazy or what?'

What's going on? I'm trying to shove through the crowd to get to her and then she staggers, arms flailing as if for balance, eyes wide with fear and then she falls. Just like that. Sinks to the ground. Crumples. The crowd hushes. It's not funny anymore.

"Dammit, get out of my way." If these fools don't move I'm going to hurt someone. I ignore the surprised looks as I kneel beside her. She's breathing. But her face is flushed and she's well and truly knocked out. I don't hesitate. I take her in my arms like I've done before and lift her. She's limp and unresponsive in my arms. Her head rests against my chest . I hope she can't hear the wild raging beat that's going nuts in there at her closeness. The crowd parts to let me pass. Their questions die away at the sight of my face. *Nobody mess with me* face. The whispers, the giggles all cut short.

I walk with Leila in my arms to the staffroom and the connected nurse's room. Except this is Samoa College and we don't have a nurse on call. Just an empty room with a bed that's far from clean. And a cupboard with no medicine in it. I don't expect to find any help in there for whatever is wrong with Leila, but for now it will have to do.

Footsteps. An eager voice behind me. "Daniel? Wait for me!" It's Sinalei. The earnest, cheerful girl that likes to follow Leila around. The really friendly one. I don't trust her though because she's with Mele far too often for comfort. I don't slow my pace. Or smile. But she runs to join me anyway. Breathless. Excited. "Is she alright? It was so strange. One minute we're walking to class and the next she starts screaming about the earth moving." A nervous giggle.

I keep walking, passing the staffroom just as Ms Sivani comes out. Concern. "What happened?"

"She had some kind of attack. Fainted in the hall." I don't pause for the teacher either. I'm not going to let Leila out of my sight. Or hand her over to anyone else. Until she opens her eyes again, she's mine. I'm in charge of her. Not her simpering friends. Not her English teacher. Nobody.

She still isn't waking up. And every minute she doesn't wake up, I get more afraid. I change my mind. I want to take her straight to my truck and up to the hospital. But Ms Sivani insists we go to the Non-existent Nurse's room first. "Maybe she just needs some air. And a rest." Because English teachers are medical practitioners in their spare time.

I take Leila there and lay her down gently on the bed. Hating the absence of her against me. Ms Sivani despatches a passing student for ice water from the staffroom. I take over when the supplies arrive. I've helped my grandmother with enough sick people to know how it's done. There's curious gossip-seekers huddling around the open doorway. I growl. "She needs air. They need to get away from here."

Ms Sivani raises an eyebrow at my tone but has to agree. She shoos the spares away while I get a cool wet cloth on Leila's forehead. And just when I'm about to curse them all and get her out of there – she starts stirring. Murmuring things I can't understand. A whimper that twists my insides.

"She's coming round." Ms Sivani exclaims. Relieved a hospital trip has been averted.

I lean forward. "Leila, are you alright?"

The moment she opens her eyes – it feels like a load has been lifted from me. I can breathe again. I can't decipher the look she gives me when she wakes up. Is she mad to see me? Is she wishing it was someone else sitting beside her? Ms Sivani wants her to go back to class, which is a stupid idea. Leila needs to go home. Lie down some more. Get out of this heat. Rest. Not keep going through this sauna of a day. Ms Sivani is normally my favourite teacher but not at that moment. But I don't have to argue with her because right then – Leila pukes. I've never been so glad to see anybody vomit before. It's difficult to hide the triumph in my voice.

"See! Leila's not ready to go back to class. I'm going to take her home myself right away." Ms Sivani is shifting into control freak teacher mode at my tone so I quickly add, "If that's alright with you."

I don't let Leila walk. Who knows when I will ever have another excuse to touch her? Hold her? Even as she protests, I sweep her up in my arms again and make my way to the truck, parked under the mango trees at the back of the school. She argues the whole way. And I don't listen to a word of it. Because all I can hear is the wild drum beat of my pulse going nuts at her closeness. And then finally she shuts up and kinda buries her face against my chest. Which feels good. I could have walked with her in my arms like this forever. (Or at least for a few miles.)

At the truck, I let her slip from my arms, testing her balance. Unwilling to let her go in case she isn't ready to stand. The stupid lock on the car door won't open at first. And when it does, I am sorry because I have no more excuses for holding her close. She won't meet my eyes. Still mad at me for carrying her. I want – no, I need – to look in her eyes. Hoping, praying she won't slap me, I raise her face to mine.

And I am lost.

Far away over miles of ocean expanse. There is solitude. The air trembles with blueness as far as the eye can see. Blue sky, blue earth. Floating there you don't know where ocean ends and where sky begins. I am so small. Insignificant in the majesty that is ocean. That is where I am as I look into your eyes. There is nothing else but us. You. Me. Nothing can reach us. Nothing can touch us. Nothing can shatter the solitude that is us. That is me and you.

I wish I could taste her. Breathe her in. And never let her go. Instead, I kiss her. Brushing my lips against her forehead.

And it is enough.

Because I am lost. In you and with you.

9

The day the whole school finds out that Leila and I are more than debate sparring enemies starts off just like any other. I don't plan it. I don't even know it's happening – as it happens.

It just does.

I find her at lunch break, moping in a corner of the school. Sad. But not just sad. On edge. Excited and freaked out all at the same time. Her mother is alive. The mother that her father told her had died eighteen years ago. Leila is a blur of emotions. Questioning everything she thinks she always knew. We talk. And she has no fences up. And no daggers ready to stab me. And there is even one trembling, breathless moment when I could have kissed her. It is right. It is a moment that cries out for her lips. But the bell rings and the moment takes a back seat. But it's still there. Breathing over my shoulder. Possibilities. Taunting me. *Are you afraid? You're afraid, aren't you! Do it. Kiss her. Can you do it?*

And when we're done talking, it seems like the most natural thing in the world to take her hand and walk with her down the hall to class. Announcing to this Samoan school community that frowns on all physical contact between boys and girls – that we are a couple. A couple that holds hands. In public. I'm guessing Leila isn't aware of the social code. But I am. Yet, I still walk with her hand in mine. Even though eyes are on us all the way to the classroom door. Even though whispers and shocked conversation follow us. I don't care. I just don't want to let her fingers, her hand out of mine.

Mine. Mine. Mine. You are mine and I am yours. Beats the rhythm of my heart.

And with that kiss still breathing over my shoulder in the back seat, taunting me - I stop her before she goes into class. Stop her and gently tug her against me, around the corner of the fast-emptying hall so no-one sees us. There's something I need to tell her. Something crucial.

"Back there when you said how alone you felt? How, without your dad, you've got no-one to trust, no-one to turn to?"

She nods. Face open and trusting. I whisper, "You're wrong. You're not alone Leila, you've got me. I don't ever want you to feel that way. You can trust me. Whenever you need me, I'm here. Just remember, you're not alone, okay?"

I want so bad for her to believe me. I wish I could tattoo the truth of it everywhere that matters. And then before she can argue with me, that unmet kiss breathing down my neck, nudges me, powers me forward, and I meet her cheek with my lips. Her skin is hot. There's a caramel sweetness in the air. Like brown sugar and fresh grated coconut, when a batch of coconut candy, *lolepopo* is bubbling on the stove. Her body is soft against mine as she leans into me. I want more. Lots more. I want to taste her lips. Hold her. Breathe into her with every piece of me. Right here, right now.

This is crazy. I gotta get out of here. I leave her. I'm fighting the urge that's growing, pulsing inside me. Knowing I have to get a whole rugby field's distance between us. Or else I won't be able to hide the fierce joy shredding me inside.

Mine. Mine. Mine. You are mine and I am yours.

I walk away, trying not to smile. A huge, goofy, foolish, smile that yells *I'm going crazy for this girl.*

And just like that, it's official. Me and Leila Folger are going out. An item. By rugby training time, she is designated as "mine".

And I don't try to argue with it.

Mine. Mine. You are mine. And I am yours.

****

That night I am riding high on the sounds of Eminem and Rihanna, when I get Simone's text.

Simone – *Soooo, share!*

*Share wat? *innocent face**

Simone – **Innocent face* my ass. U an Leila. Togethr 4eva? *wink wink**

Just friends. Good friends.

Simone – *Watevr. Evrybody knows. Sinalei saw u 2 which means the whole school wil knw by morning.*

I really like her. Esp now that she's not witching at me anymore. Nothing defn yet tho. Stil just hanging out.

Simone – *So my advice was golden?*

A little. I owe u.

Simone – *Yeah, yeah. I've heard that line b4. Empty promises and sweet lies. Jst make sure u dnt get her beat up at anymore rugby games.*

It isn't until I've signed off that it hits me. What if Leila doesn't like the school calling her my girlfriend? What if she doesn't want people to think we're going out? It's not like we discussed it or anything. Dammit. What if she gets mad? Leila mad is not an implausible thing after all. The last thing I want is for her to retreat to the #AngryGirl fortress.

I'm wary about seeing her the next day. I can't hide though. She finds me at lunch and as soon as she sees me, she's a missile honing in. I brace myself. Just in case.

She surprises me though with a gigantic grin. She's so lit up that she doesn't look like herself at all. She's talking so fast I can't make sense of anything. "Hey, slow down. I can't follow a hundred words a minute you know. Here, let's go find somewhere to sit down and you can tell me all about it. Slowly."

She tells me about going to her mother's house. (A house that sounds like it's a mansion.) A mother called Nafanua who wants to make up for lost time. She tells me she's moving in with her mother. She's giving it a go. She's excited. Happy. Unguarded.

She is beautiful.

And I can't tear my eyes off her.

She stops mid-sentence. Suspicious. "What? Why are you looking at me like that?"

"Nothing." She's suspicious though. And for Leila that's a close second to being a bitch. I blurt it out. Wishing I can take it back almost right away. "What I meant to say was, you're beautiful. Watching you talk with all the hand motions and emotions coming out everywhere. You're beautiful."

There I said it. The world can blow up now.

I had shut her up. Stunned her. Mele calls me to a prefect's meeting. I've never been so glad to hear her voice. I have to get out of here before I say anything else I might regret. *Nice one Daniel. Rip your heart out and chuck it on the ground in front of her why don't you.* I tell her I'll see her later and then I take off.

But I'm not escaping that easy. Maleko hits me with an interrogation right after the prefects meeting is finished. "So what's going on exactly with you and Leila?"

Play it down. Play it cool. "Nothing. Just hanging out."

He grins, makes a *whoop* sound of derisive doubt, and tries to shove me into the wall but I'm ready for it. I steel myself so we bump off each other instead. He laughs. "Looked like a whole lot of something to me. You got your hands full with that one. She's got some fire in her." He mimes a grinding motion against the wall as he sings. "*Wild thing, uh, you make my heart sing, you make my dick sing.*"

A rush of fury hits me. Burning red rage that shocks me with its intensity. He can tell I'm not happy because he moves away and drops the leering grin. Stops the awful singing.

I drench my voice with cold hardness. "Don't talk about her like that. Back off."

He holds his hands up in surrender, eyes wide in surprise. "Hey, I get it. Sorry. Just playing around. Chill out."

He still has that same dumbfounded look on his face when I walk away. Maleko is a friend but sometimes he's just an idiot. I don't want anyone talking about Leila and their dick in the same sentence. The sooner he gets that – the better.

10

The day drags unmercifully. I can't wait to see her. Talk to her again. About anything and everything. About nothing. Just to see her. Be with her. It makes me edgy. Difficult to concentrate in class. I meet her in the parking lot. When I see her– all the knotted rope inside me untangles. I watch her for a bit before she knows I'm here. She's frowning as she opens her car door. Frowning. What a surprise. The thick braid of hair swings lightly about her waist as she chucks her gear into the back of the shiny black Jeep. She's not as pale as she was when she first moved here. Her skin has a golden brown cast to it and even though she assures me her aunty Matile keeps forcing her to eat too much delicious Samoan food – her uniform is still a size too big and hangs on her lanky frame. I watch her and I decide.

I want Mama to meet her. Today. Now. Leila Folger is important to me. Which means I want her to meet the woman in my life who means everything to me.

I've never taken a girl to my house before. The last time I introduced a girl to Mama – I was in first grade and a bossy five year old called Bella told me I was her boyfriend. I was dutiful and introduced her as such to my grandparents when they came to Parent-Teacher interviews. Mama and Papa had been delighted to meet a feisty young woman who knew her mind at such an early age. They thought it was hilarious I had a girlfriend ordering me about. (I was very relieved when Bella's family moved away to New Zealand shortly thereafter…)

No, Leila would be the first REAL girl (who was a friend) I would take home to meet my grandmother. Mama often teased me about girls and when (if ever) was I going to start dating? I couldn't wait to see Mama's reaction to Leila.

It's nothing like I expect. Mama sees Leila in her garden and there is nothing of the kind, gentle woman that I know and love. Instead, Mama is cold. Abrupt. And when I go to help her in the kitchen, she tells me why, "Tanielu." (my Tongan name) "She is not for you."

I don't get it. "Mama, what do you mean? Leila's my friend."

"Tanielu, I mean exactly what I say. She is not for you. You would be wise to stop this friendship before it goes any further. Before it's too late. No good can come from it."

Mama is the wisest woman I know. She can mend a broken arm, soothe a fearful child sick with fever, teach an all-male group of farmers the basics of organic gardening and help a new mother usher a mewling baby into this world. This is the first time doubt has entered our relationship. "Mama, you speak in twists and turns. You've always trusted my judgement. Why not now?"

"Because there are things I know that you do not. Things I can sense, that you cannot. I speak not to hurt you, my son. Nor to cast doubt on your judgement. I tell you with a clean heart, Tanielu. That girl is not for you."

She won't be moved. And it only gets worse when Leila tells Mama who her mother is. The breaking glass is a shock to all of us but it's the look on Mama's face that really unsettles me. I've never seen her so freaked out. She's almost…afraid?

After Mama leaves us, I'm worried about how to ease the atmosphere. Leila's not clueless. There's no way she could have misinterpreted Mama's icy reception. I wouldn't blame her if she got mad and left. But she stays. She explains, "Hey, my grandmother doesn't like me so it's no big deal if yours doesn't either." A little sad that she's so used to relatives disliking her.

We spend the rest of the day in the workshop and I get to see another side to Leila that I never would have guessed at. Warrior Welder Woman. The girl is in love with the sparks, the flame, the steel – all of it. I think she likes working with blue fire more than she likes hanging out with me… Once I've shown her the basics, she zones me out. For the rest of the afternoon she is focused entirely on disc-cutting and welding the scrap metal pieces I've given her to practise on. She doesn't even notice all the times I look over at her. Studying her every move. She's changed out of her uniform into a faded pair of ripped denim shorts and a T-shirt. Clothes that are quickly covered in splatter burn holes and dirt grease smudges. She doesn't seem to care. She's oblivious to her surroundings.

I'm not. Oblivious. To her. Okay, okay, I admit it. I'm totally checking her out in those shorts – and she doesn't even notice. Those long, lean legs are impossible not to stare at. Every time she bends over to grab another piece of scrap steel, all kinds of curves scream at me. Front *and* back. Curves that are only hinted at when she's in her oversized uniform. It's getting really hot in here. And not just because of the welding heat. Or the Samoan sun.

It's a relief when it's finally time to quit. Her shirt is soaked with sweat and sticks to her skin. There's dirt marks on her face. She's breathing fast and laughing. "That was amazing! Thank you, I loved it. If you're taking on apprentices, then I'm the woman for the job."

A sudden image hits me. *Leila working on a project in my shop. Just me and her. She's all hot and bothered. She's unzipping her overalls and slowly letting them slip, slide down off her body. She's wearing the same black two-piece she had on that night in the pool. Skin glistening with sweat. She's smiling at me through the hazy smoke. Blue sparks fizz and hiss. Heat. Explosive fire.*

What is wrong with me?! I gotta get this girl out of here. She's doing things to me I can't handle.

****

It's standard practise now for us to meet up at lunch break. What's not standard is for the sight of her smile to have me on an electric high. Or for the sound of her laughter to send spider webs of pleasure down my spine. What's *really* not standard is for me to be looking for reasons – excuses – to touch her. Lean in close. Breathe her in. Kiss her cheek. But I do it anyway.

If anybody told me that one day, I would be doing an impromptu strip-show in the middle of Samoa College – I would have told them to get real. And get lost. Yet somehow, here I am. Minus my shirt, standing on a bench with students cheering me on. And with Leila flushed and laughing as she tries to tell me to stop.

I told you she does things to me I can't handle. She makes me feel things, and do things – I never would have without her.

It started with her asking me about telesa. Me telling her what little stories I knew. From there, she teased me that if she were telesa – she wouldn't ever choose to bewitch and enchant me. Which of course I took as the blatant challenge that it was. A challenge to convince her and prove otherwise. A challenge to bedazzle her with the full majesty of my awesomeness…ha. Not.

Which is how I ended up here. Maleko and the rest of the team are the loudest cheer crew. "Woohoo! Go Danny-boy, take it aallllll off! Yeah."

I flip them the finger. Discreetly. And turn back to focus on Leila. She's mortified. But not so much that she's not enjoying this. She can't stop the huge smile. The admiring glint in her eyes is at war with the embarrassment of us being the center of attention. Everything she's told me about her life back in America. Everything she hasn't told me. It all adds up to confirm for me that she's never experienced anything like this. (No, not a personal strip show!) – I mean, she's never been happy in a group of teenagers, or felt like she belongs. Here, now, with me, maybe we can change that.

She's giving me a stern face. But I've seen her angry enough times to know that she's not angry now. She looks around at the gathering crowd and turns back to me with panicked laughter in her voice, "Daniel, get down before you fall over and hurt yourself. You big show-off."

Nah, I'm having too much fun here. "No, not until you tell me what it'll take for you to hunt me down. I know. This has got to work." I start undoing the ties on my lavalava. I've got shorts on underneath but she doesn't know that.

"What the heck are you doing? Stop it. Stop it! Ohmigosh." I wish I could take a photo of her face right now. The wide-eyed stare, the horror that can't hide the happy buzz.

With a grand flourish I remove the lavalava and strike a pose. Everyone is whistling and shouting now. Over the crowd I can see Mrs Lematua look out the staffroom window, with curious disapproval about the noise. I better stop. Before I get hauled to the Principal's office. Leila grabs my hand and I let her drag me down off my stage. It's easy to fake losing my balance, grab her in my arms and collapse with her on the bench so she's sitting across my lap. She's warm, soft, laughing, happy. Chocolate pie with vanilla cream. "Okay, okay, so you win. You are disgustingly handsome, not to mention a huge show off, and any telesa would be absolutely desperate to have her way with you."

Golden sun. Green grass. Ruby red ginger flowers. Plum purple ti-leaves fluttering in the breeze. Leila in my arms. A perfect moment. I can't resist it. I ask her, "Ahh, but what about this beautiful telesa? Would you?"

She turns, her eyes meet mine. She is so close. Lush lips, hot mouth only a breath away. A whisper, "Would I what?"

Everything around us melts away. There is only us. You. Me. I want to live in this moment forever. "Choose me?"

Only two words but loaded with so much unspoken meaning. I am poised at the edge of a waterfall. Waiting. Wondering. What will she say?

"Yes. I would."

And just like that.

I fall some more.

11

Why is that guys are supposed to have kissed tons of girls – or else they're designated "losers"? While girls are supposed to only have kissed one or two people at the very most - or else they're designated "sluts"? That never made much sense to me at all. But then there's a lot about kissing. And girls. That has always eluded me.

When guys get together they like to talk about girls. Which usually leads to talking about who they've been kissing lately. Or wanting to kiss lately. Me? I like to adopt a 'man of mystery' approach to the whole thing. I tell them that according to my Grandfather, 'a gentleman never kisses and tells.' Which of course makes it sound like I'm getting it on with loads of girls. Ha. When really? The truth? I've only ever kissed two girls. And I'm not sure forced mouth-mashing actually qualifies. Samantha Matu kissed me in Year 5 when the girls were playing 'Chase the boys and Kiss Them.' (Okay, so she was a faster runner than me, but damn, have you seen her? That girl is a giant compared to the rest of us and nobody could escape her. The kiss she plastered on my clamped shut lips was vicious.) My second kiss wasn't much better. In Year 8 a girl called Malia liked me. So her best friend told Maleko to tell me that I should meet Malia at the back of the school hall. Well, I did and after standing there in total silence for ten minutes (while Maleko made faces at me from around the corner, egging me on) we both had the same idea and kind of smushed our lips together for all of two seconds. Which left me wondering, 'what the heck is the big deal with kissing anyway?'

The day I kiss Leila gives me the answer to that question – and then some. We go running together at the SamCo field and she basically kills me in the fitness and endurance department. (*Shh, don't tell Coach.*) It's getting dark by the time we're done, so the field is empty. Just me and her with the stars coming out. She's wearing blue running shorts and a white singlet with this black sports halter top kinda thing inside it. She's flushed, sweaty and laughing, really loving the fact that she just kicked my ass on the track. She smiles up at me. That's all it takes and everything comes to a crashing halt, like someone has taken me out with a killer tackle. No air. No sound. Nothing. Why has the world stopped? Why can't I breathe or move or feel anything?

I look at her. *Really* look at her.

I've seen Leila without a shirt before, so I know that under the clothes she wears with awkward unease – there's a body that dips and curves in all the right places. In unforgettable ways. (And believe me, ever since the night I surprised her at the pool, I've been trying *not* to remember it.) It's easier when she's in the orange and yellow school uniform every day, but tonight, her workout clothes cling to her with sweat in a way that I bet would make her really mad if she knew. I try to focus just on her eyes - but my brain is filling in all the tantalizing gaps. There is so much about her that is familiar now. So much about her that I can shut my eyes and trace her from memory.

The legs that go on forever. The slight slouch to her shoulders because she's always trying to hide that she's taller than most everyone around her. Her gangly arms that she waves around all over the place when she's trying to get her point across. The thick rope of hair that I wish I could loosen from its braid, just so I can see if the sandy highlights will catch fire in the moonlight. Her black onyx eyes that can knife through a guy if he's dumb enough to debate with her. Or soften to a midnight ocean velvet when memories entangle her. Or glint with chipped diamonds of laughter when she's teasing me…*Are you sure you're man enough to risk losing a race to a girl? I think I saw you struggling to keep up there for a few laps.*

Damn. She's beautiful.

Everything about Leila both intrigues and infuriates me. From her anger to the sadness that she drowns in when she talks about her Dad to her ever-readiness to believe the worst of me. Any encounters with Leila inevitably have me feeling like I want to smash stuff. Or like I need to go for a long, hard swim in an icy cold pool. Or both.

But tonight, Leila isn't making me mad. Or confused. She's just smiling and laughing and talking. And being so damn beautiful that it hurts. A lot. In my chest. My head. And everywhere else that a guy feels stuff.

We sit and talk but I'm not focusing on the words coming out of my mouth. Because every piece of me is caught up in her. She sits beside me on grass that's still warm from the fast fading day. We're barely close enough to touch but every breath I take tastes of her. The savor of roasted koko beans with lots of brown sugar. And hints of vanilla spiced with the burn of chilli. Why does she always remind me of chocolate? We talk but all I can think about is how beautiful she looks in the moonlight. And wonder... *how angry would she be if I tried to kiss her*?

And then she runs her fingers along my shoulder, tracing the patterns of the tattoo on my arm. Her touch burns. It's a struggle not to jump up and run a mile in the opposite direction. Because I want to touch her back. Hold her. Taste her mouth on mine. And I know I can't. Shouldn't.

For the barest of moments, I try to halt the tidal wave of heat that's sweeping me towards her. I try. (Honest. I'm not kidding.) And then I'm not trying anymore. Because then a thought, a longing has melded into a moment. I breathe a kiss on her cheek. Sweet edged with the salt of sweat. And then her lips are opening under mine.

I'm sinking, melting, drowning in a pool of hot chocolate. Everything splinters into flashes. A swirling kaleidoscope.

Hot. Mouth. Velvet sky. Stars gleaming. Tongue. Searching. Hands. Tugging my hair. Skin against skin. Hard. Sweat. Pulse. Hot. Electrical current wired from earth to heavens. Heart beat. Sweet. Hot. Fire. Raging. Kiss. Faraway ocean roars. Crash. Foam. Leila. Hot. Hot. Fire. Hot.

Too hot. Shit! Ouch.

"Leila, what's happening?"

She pushes me from her with a strength I didn't know she had. "Daniel, get away from me!"

And then, the girl who has set me on fire with a kiss – explodes and bursts into flames.

****

'I hurt you tonight Daniel. And I'm sorry. I never want to do that again. Let me go. Nafanua will be worried and I don't know how to explain this to her. I'm tired. I don't want to be with you anymore. I shouldn't have kissed you. It wasn't what I wanted. This – you – me – it's not going to work. I don't want it to. I just want us to be friends, that's all. Just let me go, okay?'

The words replay in my mind, over and over again. Her voice – cold and emotionless. Her face – blank of anything familiar. Not even the trademark Leila anger. Just nothing. We kiss. She blows up and sets fire to the place. I take her home. And then she tells me it's over. Asks me to leave. We're finished. Before we even started.

But it's too late. Because I've already fallen.

Over the edge into that roaring, surging chasm of foam. Torn and tossed by fierce turbulent currents beyond my control. Swept along by a river of emotion that rushes me to the vast sea. I am drowning.

I don't get it. One minute life is full of perfect possibilities.

The next minute – it totally sucks.

****

She doesn't show up to school that whole week. I call her. More times than I'll admit - even to myself. She never picks up. I call her mother's house and the housekeeper never puts me through. *I'm sorry, Leila is sleeping… I'm sorry Leila is not taking any phone calls… I'm sorry Leila doesn't wish to speak to anyone… I'm sorry.* She doesn't sound sorry at all. Witch.

Simone is no use. He doesn't know what's going on either. Leila's not answering his calls. She texts him some B.S about 'busy dealing with a family emergency.' He gives me a pitying glance, "You know what family fa'alavelave's can be like. She's caught up in one. Don't worry. She'll be back to school soon. And you two will be back on."

No. This has nothing to do with family funerals or weddings or any other kind of Samoan family drama. And everything to do with her catching on fire when we kissed.

That kiss. It haunts me. I dream about it – and they aren't always good dreams either. Me. Leila. Her lips on mine. Drowning and then exploding. Sometimes the dreams are a mixed up tangle of water and fire. Sometimes the scene changes and we're making out in the sea and the water ocean goes nuts around us. None of it makes sense. I'm going to the pool at Faatoia every night. Maybe because I'm hoping she'll be there. Maybe because the cool water is calling to me even louder, even stronger than it did before. Swimming there eases the ache. Calms the confused mess that's tearing me up inside.

At first I thought she was avoiding me because she's embarrassed about what happened. And then as the days go on, I realize that's not it. She doesn't want to see me again because she regrets that kiss. She regrets taking that step out of the friend zone. I don't get it. Her smile. Her voice. Her hand in mine. Everything told me that she felt the same things I did. Didn't she?

I have to see her.

Drive up to the tall white house in the middle of nowhere. An old woman answers the door. It's not Leila's mother. Some of the boys had seen her mother the day she came to pick her up from school and they couldn't stop talking about her. And her car. *You should have seen her, she was sex on stilettos.* I'd never seen her but it made my skin crawl to listen to the boys talk. Because she was Leila's mother and mother's weren't supposed to be sex on stilettoes…

No this severe looking woman definitely isn't Nafanua. This woman doesn't smile and she looks even more sour when I ask for Leila.

"She's asleep." No apologies. No offer to take a message. Nothing.

A lesser man would have been put off. But there's a reason why teachers and students alike find it difficult to stay mad at me for long. Mama always says Charm is my middle name. Here we go…My half-smile. Just a hint of pleading in my eyes. Lean forward in a conspiratorial closeness. "Is she really asleep? Or is she just trying to avoid me?"

The woman takes a step backward, narrows her eyes at me, folds her arms across her chest. "I don't know. I'm not her secretary. You're the boy who keeps calling." Still no smile. This one will be tough to crack.

Sad face. Appealing for sympathy. (I'm beginning to think she might not have a heart though, so perhaps there's nothing to appeal to.) "Yes, I'm the one who's been calling." Well, I'm *hoping* I'm the only boy who's choking up the phone line… "I hope you can help me. You see, I care about her. She hasn't been to school all week and me and the rest of her friends are worried."

"She's fine. Don't worry." No, the woman is still not budging.

"All I want is to talk to her for five minutes then I'll get off your doorstep. I'm not leaving until I see her. Please?"

Before she can tell me again to get out, I see Leila come down the stairs. She looks like hell. Washed out and washed up. "Leila, what's going on? Are you okay? I've been worried about you."

Her face is hard. Closed. "You shouldn't be here. I'm fine, really I am. You don't need to worry about me. I've been a bit sick, but it's no big deal and I should be back at school next week. You should go. I'm sure you have lots of stuff to do at the workshop."

She's brushing me off. Talking shit about school and being sick. She expects me to just leave after hearing that? She's lying. She has to be. I walk over to her. Wanting to shake her. Make her see there's no way she can lie to me after her lips have burned me to the core. But instead, I just hold her. "Don't do this. What happened the other night, we need to talk about it. I need to know if you're alright. I need to know what's going on. Don't shut me out like this."

She's calm. Cool. But not confident. This close to her and I taste an edge to the air. It's fear. This isn't the same girl I kissed under wakening stars. This girl is terrified and it's making her defensive-aggressive. What's she afraid of? She hides her eyes from me. Hides the truth. I raise her face to mine. She's trying not to breathe too fast. Her skin is too hot against my fingers but I'm not letting her go. *Go ahead, set this place on fire – I'm not running. I'm not letting you go.* "Leila, don't do this. What happened the other night, we need to talk about it. I need to know if you're alright. I need to know what's going on. Don't shut me out like this."

There is a moment when she almost decides to let me in. I see it in her eyes. Bending, wilting, opening. *Let me in.* A white sandy expanse of beach beckons. It stretches ahead of us for miles. Golden and blue with promise. With light feet of freedom. *Let me in Leila. Walk with me. Together. Please.*

And then that moment is gone. Shut down by the tight, stony wall of resolve. "This is ridiculous. What makes you think you can come in here and make me talk to you when I don't want to? I'm not like one of your puppy dog rugby players ready to run and ruck whenever you tell them to. I have nothing to say to you. I want you to leave."

Every word out of her mouth now is vicious. Angry. She turns away. I catch at her hand. Her skin is so hot that I flinch. But still, I'm not ready to let go. Steel determination. "Nothing Leila? Do you really have nothing to say to me?"

Her reply isn't what I was hoping for. "You're a really nice guy, but I'm sorry, I don't think we should hang out anymore. We both have stuff going on and it would be better if we just stopped this before someone got hurt…." The words keep going. A relentless tidal wave. A whole lot of words about why we shouldn't be together. Why we shouldn't have hooked up in the first place. A whole lot of rubbish. All of it.

I stare at her, looking for cracks in the armour. But there aren't any. She means every poison-filled word. I ask, "That's all you're going to say about the other night, about what happened? That's it?"

"Yes, that's it. We both know that I've got a problem and I need help to fix it. I'm glad you helped me the other night and I would appreciate it if you could keep it a secret. I'm working on doing something about it."

Dammit. I don't care about the fire thing. What about the kiss Leila? What about the coiled wire of electricity that is binding me to her even now? Even now as she rages at me. "I'm not talking about you bursting into flames. I'm talking about you and me. Us. Our friendship. We kissed. I'm talking about what's going on between you and me. Don't tell me to just forget us."

That makes her snap even more. Now she's screaming. "That's exactly what I'm saying. There is no us. We aren't an 'us'. It's impossible. And it's the last thing I want right now so would you please just leave? Before I ask Netta to call the police or something?" She shoves me away from her, two hands to my chest. Hard. "Just get out, okay? Go away!"

I move back because it's the right thing to do. When a girl hates the sight of you that much, that's what you do. You get the hell out of her way.

She runs out the side doors, down the veranda steps and over the stretch of grass. Leaving me staring after her. A fool. Who had been dumb enough to think that a kiss meant something.

12

The weeks without Leila are the busiest of my life. I don't want a single spare minute free to waste on thinking about her. Early mornings are for training. School gets my full attention. No mucking around. A few people ask me about Leila but they quickly stop asking when I give them nothing. Lying is easy when the truth is too hard. "I'm not sure. I think she's gone back home to the US. She was only here for a short while anyway."

Only Simone's eyes tell me that he knows the truth. But I don't worry. Me and Simone have an understanding. I keep his secrets and he keeps mine. I have his back and he has mine.

I take on another steel fabrication job at work, hire temporary sub-contractors and organize them into two teams so we can work constant shifts around the clock. As soon as school is out, I go straight to work. You can't think about girls when you're welding. You might burn a hole in your leg. Or make a mistake that costs you thousands. There is no room for thoughts of Leila and hot kisses in a workshop filled with smoke, welding fumes and the screech of a grinder. I lead the team that installs the warehouse we have fabricated. There is no room for thoughts of Leila and her challenging stare on site. Her laugh. The light of her smile. Not when I'm thirty feet in the air, stepping from one steel girder to the next, hanging on with one arm and welding with the other.

Most nights I get home so late, so tired – that all I have energy left for is to shovel food in my mouth and collapse into bed. Exhaustion is good for nightmares. Because no matter how bad they get, you never wake up. Until it's morning and it's time to chase the clock again. I have no time for music. No energy for visits to the Faatoia pool. No will for song writing. I have plenty of power for rugby though. It's my one release. Explosive. Powerful. I keep getting cited for dangerous tackles. Rough play. Abusing the referee. Finally the coach benches me. Tries to give me "the talk". Probing for answers, 'w*hat's wrong?'*

Nothing. There is nothing wrong with me.

Because Leila's gone. And all I need is time to re-align myself. Time to fill in the jagged spaces she's hacked into me. For the first time in my life, I can understand Eminem like I never have before.

And then Mele breaks up with Maleko because she's tired of his endless flirting with every girl he can get to smile at him. She's waiting for me one day when I come out of the library. She's been crying. Girls and tears – a bad combination designed to make you do things you don't want to...

"Daniel, can I talk to you please?" Tears make black lines of drowned mascara on her cheeks.
No, I don't want to talk . I want to be anywhere but here. Is what I want to say. But don't.
I say nothing instead. And I try to smile.

She takes that as an encouraging sign and grabs at my arm. "We've been friends for a long time…"

We have? I wouldn't call being trapped in the same classroom for the last five years – 'friends.' But now is not the time to argue semantics. Because she's crying even more. And clutching at my arm like it's a life raft. I'd rather face a take-down by the Leififi rugby team than be caught by a crying girl. *Not true Daniel.* I get a flash back to another crying girl. Sitting beside a black pool. Wanting to hold her. Kiss her tears away. *F***, stop it.* Leila's gone. And I'm not wasting any time thinking about her.

I smile down at Mele. Pat her on the shoulder. We sit down. "Can I help you with something?"

"Oh Daniel, what's wrong with me?" she is so bewildered, so sad that it's a wail.

What's wrong with you? *Well, sometimes you're shallow and vicious and obsessed with cutting other people to shreds –but apart from that, there's nothing wrong with you.* Somehow I don't think that's the answer she's looking for. "There's nothing wrong with you. Why?"

Another sniff. "Am I fat? Ugly? Am I a horrible girlfriend? What is it? I don't get it. I try my best to make Maleko happy and he keeps messing around with other girls. What's wrong with me?"

More tears. And this time, they get to me. Because I know Maleko. And yes, he is a player. Or at least, he tries to be. He's a minor miracle man because in a place where everyone gets strictly chaperoned everywhere - he has managed to have sex with a surprising number of willing and eager girls. Without their parents or pastors finding out. Mele sobs into my shoulder and I feel sorry for her. For all her irritating ways, she had been very committed to Maleko. I'd expected her to be sick of him long before this.

"Hey, you're not ugly. Or fat. Or any of that stuff. You're very pretty. And you always look good." I wasn't lying so I didn't stumble over the words. If there's one girl who always looks good, it's Mele. I don't think I've ever seen her sweaty, messy, or less than perfectly put together – until now. *Another flashback. Leila in her underwear. Wet. Sticky. Leila in her running gear. Sweaty. Bushy hair coming undone from its braids. Leila cutting grass in her school uniform. Dirty face. Grass stains on her skirt. Leaves in her hair. Leila puking in a rubbish can.*

Leila. Nothing like Mele. Leila. Different from Mele in every way.

And I want her so bad it hurts.

Mele has to repeat her question twice because I'm not paying attention to her. "I said, why do you suppose Maleko isn't satisfied with me then. Seeing as how you think I'm beautiful." She lowers her voice and moves closer.

I never said you were beautiful. 'Pretty' is a world of difference from beautiful. But it's too late to back out now. I shrug. "Because Maleko is an idiot." That's true too.

Mele stares at me with big, hopeful eyes. "You always know how to make me feel better. Thank you Daniel."

Then out of nowhere, she leans forward and aims a kiss at my mouth. I jerk to the left and manage to evade most of it so she lands on my chin instead. Oh shit. I knew I shouldn't have let her corner me like this. She holds my face firmly in her hands so she can look into my eyes, "Boys like you are honest. And they don't play around with a girl's feelings. We've always shared a special bond, haven't we?"

Alarm bells. What bond? Somebody rescue me please. Get me out of this.

"Remember that time when Maleko was teasing me about my English essay and you told him to leave me alone? And that time he was flirting with the St. Mary's College girl and you told him he should be nicer to me?"

Yeah, I remember. And now I wish I hadn't said those things. Because she's looking at me with hungry eyes. This is what happens when you try to be a nice guy. Pretty, determined girls want to sink their hooks into you. Next time, just keep your mouth shut Daniel.

I'm not saying anything but that doesn't bother a girl like Mele. She keeps going. "You've always been different. You've always had a special place in my heart."

She heaves a deep sigh that accentuates the chest that she's pressing into my arm. I'm dying here. The bell goes, saving me from this awkwardness. She lets go of me and stands up. "I have to go. We'll talk more again later. Bye!"

There are no more tears - only triumph - as she smiles at me and walks away. Her swagger mojo is back. I watch her go. She flicks her hair over one shoulder and throws me one more smile. It says, *I am gorgeous and I know you're looking at me. I know you want me.* It's a look that Leila would never give anyone. For some reason that thought makes me mad. Leila would never smile like that at me anyway because she's not interested in going out with me. She's made that very clear. Mele is pretty. And she's willing. Available. You would have to be a fool to turn her down.

And I'm tired of being a fool.

****

It happens gradually without any planning or thought. Not from me anyway. I go to early-morning training and Mele's there on the side-lines. Studying, while her Dad has us go through drills. She's not there for Maleko anymore so the team is all wondering who she IS there for. I spend lunch break in the library and she finds me there. She doesn't try to talk much. Just finds a seat close to mine and gets into her books. We don't ever plan to be there together. But it's enough for people to start making assumptions. Whispers and jokes about me and Mele being an item now. I don't try to shut them down. I have other things on my mind.

Like trying to forget about a girl on fire.

****

Weeks pass. Nobody's heard from her. My grandmother has stopped giving me worried, fretful glances. Even Simone isn't bugging me about the Mele rumours. He's still making vomit faces behind her back every time he sees her talking to me though. "We're not dating." I tell him. Again.

"So? She's fantasizing that you are." Is his rude response.

I don't care. I'm beyond caring about any girl, anymore. I'd already tried that once and it hadn't worked out so well for me. By my estimate, Leila has gone back to America by now. Back to her fast life of fast food and rich white people who didn't like her.

And then, one sweltering Saturday – there she is. Sitting in the front seat of a big red Ford truck. Smiling, laughing with the driver. Some blonde man. They've pulled up to a red light. She doesn't see me. But I see her. She looks happy. Light. Free. A thousand miles away. From me. From us. Happy with a stranger.

All those times I said I was over her? All those times I said I don't care anymore? - Lies. All of them. Because when the light turns green and they drive away.

I die inside.

13

I walk into Geography class and Leila is sitting there - like she'd never left. Her head is bent over her books, face turned away but I know instantly who it is. The curve of her neck, the thick untamed hair. She looks over at me. Unsmiling. Walls up in her eyes. And then she looks away. Cool. Calm. Composed. As if she hasn't seen me. As if I am nothing more than another face in a crowd.

Anger simmers in me, slow but sure. What is she doing back? Where has she been? What has she been doing – besides ride around in trucks with strange white guys? Why is she here now? Does she suspect what kind of nightmare I've been living in ever since she kicked me out of her mother's house? Does she even care? I wish she hadn't reappeared. I want her to go and be gone forever. Rage builds like a rising tide.

After class, we meet in the hall. I'm tempted to race off in the opposite direction I'm not going to let her see how she affects me. Hell no. *You ripped my heart out and stomped on it. It's only just starting to heal. You being here is shredding it all over again. Why can't you go back to America so I won't have to hurt like this?* Is what I want to say. But don't. "Leila."

Her tone matches mine. Impersonal. Two acquaintances passing in the street. "Daniel."

I'm polite. "How are you?"

She's polite. "Fine thanks."

There are eyes boring into my back. The gossip wire is buzzing, waiting for fuel so it can catch fire. "So you're back."

"Yeah. Back to school."

"For how long?" Did you think of me over these past weeks? At all? Do you regret breaking up with me? Ever? Are you still catching on fire when you kiss people? Cancel that. I don't want to know if you've been kissing anybody.

She looks confused. I explain. "How long? How long are you back for? Don't you head back home to the States soon?"

She shakes her head. Still distant. Still cool. Still an ocean away. "No. Plans have changed. I'm sticking around for a while. Probably a long while." She sounds bored at the prospect. Why are you sticking around when it's obvious you hate it here. Hate us. Hate me.

We both go quiet. Politeness can only carry you so far. Questions are churning inside me, battling to escape. *Why did you kiss me like that if you didn't care? Why did you lie to me? Why did you make me think that you cared? Why did you laugh with me – if I didn't make you happy? Was I just a phase? Why did you catch on fire? Who was that?*

Move on Daniel. Walk away. Don't stand here like a dumbass. She's going to see you're hurting. She's going to know. Move!

And then Mele saves me. "Danny, you'll be late for practise. I'm waiting for you." I've never been so glad to see a girl I don't like. She grabs my hand, pulling me away, and I let her. Saved by the siren.

As soon as we're out of sight, I carefully slip my hand out of Mele's, giving her a grateful smile. "Thanks."

For once, the girl doesn't give me her *I-Am-Sex* smile. Just shrugs. "You looked like you needed rescuing. What else are friends for?" She looks so sad to say the word 'friends' that I stop her. Have to say it.

"Hey, I am grateful. That we're friends. And I'm sorry it can't be…more."

In an unusual moment of honesty, without the façade of flirtatiousness, she replies, "Why can't we be more? You saw her. She doesn't want you back. Why are you still hung up on her?"

Hold up. Rewind. I don't like *this* much honesty. "I'm not. We were only hanging out for a little while. I'm not into her."

She rolls her eyes at me in a move that reminds me of Simone. "Oh please, if there's one thing I'm good at, it's knowing when a boy is hot for me. Or – in this case – hot for someone else. You are so in to her, it's disgusting. I don't know why. She's not even pretty."

No, Leila isn't pretty. Leila is something else entirely. Something Mele could never be. Or understand. But now is not the time to get into it because Mele has just rescued me from an awkward moment. I smile at her, "Come on, let's go. I'll buy you lunch. To say thanks for the save back there."

If I play it right, I won't have to run into Leila again. That feels good and it hurts all at the same time.

****

But the stars are not in alignment. Because we have Culture Night practise and who rocks up to Williams House with Simone? #Angry Girl. This is worse than a nightmare. How am I supposed to dance and sing - knowing she'll be watching? Knowing how she ***doesn't*** feel about me?

All through the singing practise, I sense her. Without even looking at her, I knew where she is. Even though I don't want to. And then it's time for our war dance. I strip off my shirt and let discomfort turn into anger. Screw her. This is my school. My war dance. Let her see what she's missing out on. Let her see what she screamed at '*Get away from me*."

I take my position in the front and call for the boys to be ready, "Sauni!"

The drums start and I pour everything into the motions. Anger. Defiance. Rage. Screw you Leila Folger. I am strength. Passion. Energy. Movement. Dance. I am Warrior.

The drum beats fade, leaving me standing there, drenched in sweat under a blazing sun, every piece of me triumphant. Alive. Adrenaline pumping. Screw girls who change into psycho bitches the minute they get you to fall in love with them.

The word *love* hits me over the head like a steel beam. *Shut up. Get lost. Who said anything about love?* I'm not in love. I can't be. Not with her. Not now. Not ever.

It's the girls turn to dance. Leila doesn't join them. She sits in the shade and watches while the rest of the girls perform their siva. Of course. The American girl doesn't know how to Samoan siva. Simone is doing a good job of outshining the girls though. I whistle for him at the end of the performance and he gives me the finger before saucily strutting back to sit beside Leila.

"Daniel, can we run through your song now?" Ms Lematua calls for me. No, I don't want to sing about love and heartache right now. Not when the girl who broke my heart is sitting there listening.

"Sure." I grab my guitar and strum it for a little bit, calming the racing pulse. Cool it Daniel. Don't let her rattle you. Show her you don't care. Show her you're okay. The song is one I've written specially for the performance. It tells the story of Sina and the

Dolphin Warrior. One of those tragic legends that has all the girls sighing and us boys rolling our eyes and gagging.

I sing the same song I've been singing every day for practise over the last two weeks, but today it's different. Today it means something. Today I am Vaea who had been dumb enough to fall in love with a girl he couldn't have. Loved her so hard it caused a war and general mayhem. Loved her so bad he gave up everything to be with her. Loved her so hard that losing her drove him to give up being human just so he could be with her. Yeah, I sing that song and for the first time, I know exactly what the words mean. I know exactly how Vaea feels.

I AM DANIEL TAHI.

14

We have a game today so I can't waste any time thinking about the unwelcome realization that *maybe*, I'm in love with Leila Folger. Must focus. I'm looking forward to smashing people. I hope it hurts. A lot.

I can't find Maleko after school. Usually he gets a ride with me to games but he's nowhere to be found so I go on without him. The game is at Pesega School fields. The last thing I expect to see as I turn in at the gate - is a familiar black Wrangler. Leila? At a rugby game? Yes! She must want to see me. It seems too good to be true. But why else would she be here? She hates rugby. She could only be here because she wants to talk. I pull up beside the Wrangler. Trying not to smile. *Play it cool. Play it calm.* I look over.

I'm wrong about the jeep being the last thing I expect to see today. Because the last thing I expect to see EVER is happening right there in front of me. Maleko is sitting in the front seat beside Leila. No strike that, Leila is practically sitting in his lap. He has his arm around her and his face all up in hers. What's going on? It looks like they're having fully-clothed sex right here in the parking lot. Have you ever been hit by a truck? I haven't either. But I can tell you what it must feel like. Try doing a belly flop into the sea from a twenty foot high drop. Try having an entire rugby team jump on you. That's how it feels, seeing Leila get her freak on with Maleko.

Maleko jumps to his feet when he sees me. “Hey Danny, Leila’s Wrangler beat you here, ay? You better retire the green bomb.”

I’m going to kill you. Rip your head off and grind your face into the dirt. Get your punk ass out of her car. I smile. “I didn’t realize Leila was providing a taxi service to rugby games now or else I would have hitched a ride too”

I get out of the truck. I’m proud to say I don’t slam the door. Maleko relaxes. The fool actually believes my performance. He sits back down beside Leila and that arm goes around her shoulders.

Get your filthy hands off her you piece of shit. I’m going to tear that arm out of its socket. Use it to beat you senseless.

Maleko’s smile needs to get wiped off his face. “What do you think, is Coach going to let me play Wing today?”

As if. What are you? Digby Ioane from the Australian Wallabies Rugby team? “I don’t know, you were kinda slow at practise yesterday man. I think a game against Avele College needs someone with a bit more speed and power, you know.”

Maleko gets out of the car. I don’t need to rip him out piece by piece. “Whatever man! Coach knows I’m ready for it. Today’s the day, I’m sure of it.”

Yeah, today is your day alright. Not. Over my dead body. I’m seething so bad with rage that I can’t see straight. Maleko needs to get far away from me. Quickly. How can he be hooking up with Leila so fast? What happened to all that crap about it being too dangerous for her to be with anyone? Yeah, anyone except white boys who drive red trucks. Anyone except Maleko. I deserve an Academy award for my epic acting skills here. “So, Leila, you coming to watch the game today? I guess you want to check out Maleko’s moves on the field?”

She has the grace to look uncomfortable now. Maleko answers before she does. “Nah, she said she doesn’t want to get beat up again. I think you ruined all rugby games for her.”

Okay that hurts. I flash back without wanting to. *Leila’s fear as she’s shoved around in the rioting crowd. Her face after that boy hits her. The way she reels. Her confusion. Panic*. And then like the floodgates have been opened, everything else comes rushing back. All the things I’ve been trying to lock away. Me and her by the pool. Laughing. Me and her talking for hours. Teasing her with a strip show. Watching her run. Kissing her under the starry sky. And then her screaming at me to leave her alone. Running away from me. Cutting me loose.

Yeah, it definitely hurts. “Of course. I understand. Your first rugby game was not something you would want to remember. It didn’t turn out the way it was supposed to, the way I wanted it to.”

Maleko gives me a questioning look. But it’s Leila who rushes to fill in the awkward silence. “No, it didn’t, but I didn’t care. It didn’t matter. I mean I liked that day. Oh whatever!”

What’s she trying to say now? That she liked getting her face smashed? Or that I shouldn’t feel bad about it because she doesn’t care either way? I stare at her. She looks angry now as she gets out of the Jeep. “Maleko’s wrong. He doesn’t know anything about what I want. I’m staying to watch the game. Of course I am.”

That’s probably the truest thing I’ve heard her say yet. Because not only does Maleko not know what she wants, neither do I. And somehow, I’m getting the feeling that she doesn’t know what the hell she wants either.

We both watch as she walks away towards the field. Maleko swears and mutters, “What’s her problem?”

I turn to him. “What are you doing with her anyway?”

He fakes an innocent look. “We’re just hanging out. No big deal.” A sly grin. “She’s single. She’s hot. And she hasn’t yet experienced the awesomeness that is Maleko the Master.”
He trots off, but not before throwing over his shoulder. “Hey, don’t worry. We can share. When I’m done you can have her back.” A whoop of laughter that isn’t funny.

I am going to kill you.

Several deep breaths later and I join the rest of the team. Coach is going over the game plan but I’m distracted, trying to see Leila without making it obvious that I’m looking for her. Ah, there she is. Standing with Mele on the side-lines. Both of them looked pissed off. Maleko is loudly telling the others about Leila. Snatches of conversation. Admiring jeers. Maleko is revelling in it.

‘And then I said to her, we could make beautiful music together…ahhh she couldn’t handle all of this anyway!’ Boisterous laughter. ‘Make sure you all make me look good today, she’s here to watch me play. I’m going to have a SBW wardrobe malfunction. She’ll probably run onto the field and try to jump me right there…’

This has gone too far. The world goes ice cold in the sun-burnt afternoon as I move towards him, already seeing the world implode with blood as I imagine landing a punch. Breaking his nose. Wiping that smile off his face. But before I can make it happen, the whistle blows for the game to start. Coach orders everyone on the field. I move on autopilot still wanting to break his face. Hurt him. Shut him up.

I want everything around me to mirror the hurt inside.

The game begins. But it’s inevitable. An explosion waiting to happen. Maleko brushes against me during a scuffle for the ball and that’s the only catalyst required. Rage unleashes. It’s not right, I know. It’s not mature, responsible or especially Captain-like. But I do it. I hit him. Maleko’s caught off guard but not for long. And then we’re on the ground, at each other’s throats. Dirt. Heat. Sweat. Mud. Grass. Blood. Rage. Saliva. Fist connecting. Red haze

- as red as the metallic burn of blood in my mouth. Blue thirst - as blue as the dazed drowning sensation I am struggling in as I try to hurt the boy who has been my friend ever since Grade One.

When they finally manage to break us apart, I get even angrier. Because I'm not done. I haven't had enough. I still hurt. I still want to rage, rage and burn until I can't feel anything anymore. But as they pull me away with the Coach shouting at us both, all I can see is her. Leila. Standing there with a blank look on her face. As devoid of emotion as when I caught her making out with Maleko. All I can see is her.

And it hurts.

****

They don't need to order me off the field. Nothing could have kept me there. I get in my truck and drive. Am I running away? I drive without purpose. I drive, taking the coastal road and as I drive, I feel the hum of the blue-ness that twines alongside the route and it calms me. Soothes me. And after a long time of mindless driving, I pull into a lonely strip of sand edging a wild rocky clash of white foam. It's not a beach for swimming. But it's perfect for thinking. Angry thoughts. About girls who hurt you. And friends who are dumb enough to hit on girls that hurt you. The surf crashing on the black rocks looks like how I feel. There is something meditative about watching the ocean. Letting its relentless waves wash over your mind. I sit there until the sun dies. Long enough for anger to get lost. And reason to set in. With logic comes guilt. Shame. Shouldn't have lost it like that. Need to accept the facts.

Fact number one - If love is a gut-wrenching ache, a cliff-jumping rush, a want…a *need* to live and breathe the same air as her always – then yeah, I'm in love with Leila.

Fact number two – She doesn't love me back. Leila and I are never going to be together. It doesn't matter how much I feel like she's a part of me. Or how bad it hurts to not have her.

Fact number three – Facts one and two suck.

Time to go home. I'm sore all over. Stinking of sweat. Mama's waiting for me. Concerned. "Where have you been? Why are you so late?"

"Late game." I got nothing else to offer her. She's never approved of Leila. She was relieved when I told her that she had stopped coming to school. She wouldn't be happy now to know Leila's back.

Mama's eyes narrow. "What are those bruises? Did you get into a fight?"

"Rough game but I'm fine." Lies. I'm not fine. I don't know if I ever will be.

Injuries are the perfect distraction for a healer. Mama goes to work with her ointments and medicines. I let her fuss over me, grateful she's not bugging me for specifics of the day's bust-up. I need all the kindness I can get because tomorrow I'll have to go through the torture again of seeing the girl I love - laugh and talk to someone else.

Nice one Daniel. Next time you want to fall in love? Check to make sure the girl actually gives a shit about you first.

15

I got my day planned out. I'm going to find Coach and apologize. Resign as Captain of the team. Then go see the Principal and hand in my badge. Take responsibility for my actions. But Maleko gets to school before me. Him and his black eye are waiting for me outside Coach's office. He whispers, "Go with it." By the time I meet with Coach, it's so he can tell me that Maleko's already explained the fight, taken the blame for riling me up.

Coach is stern, "He told us about the derogatory remarks he was making about your family. Unacceptable behaviour and very disappointing from boys who are supposed to be teammates and have each other's back. He's been benched." A pause, "I'm still surprised with you though Daniel. I wouldn't expect you to be so easily provoked." I'm lucky. We've got a championship coming up and Coach doesn't want to lose either of his two best players so we get off lightly. We're not getting referred to the Principal. We both have to apologize to the rest of the team and then clean Coach's office.

Maleko meets me when I leave the office. He looks way worse than I do. That makes me feel better about life in general. Even though I know it shouldn't. He doesn't smile. Just takes a deep breath before mumbling, "Hey man, I'm sorry. I was out of line. I would never have tried anything if I thought you two were still on."

"We're not on."

He shrugs. “Whatever you say. Are we cool?” Hopeful.

I smile at his black eye. “I should be asking you that. Your face looks bad. Are we cool?”

His shoulders sag with relief. “Yeah. We cool.” The requisite hand shake and shoulder-lock and everything really is cool.

****

Everyone and everything seemed to be conspiring against me. Against my goal to not get stuck with Leila anywhere. I’m not happy when I walk into the deserted classroom. She’s sitting at a desk in the corner with her head down, focusing on her book. She looks up. A pained smile. “Hi.”

Hi yourself. Do you know what it’s like to have someone’s smile, someone’s voice - stuck in your head on constant replay? Imprinted so deep into your brain that you can’t get them out? A someone who’s not interested in even having you around as a friend? No? Well, let me tell you what it feels like.

It bites. Big time.

I sit down opposite her at the desk. I’m supposed to rush through this, get the torture over as quick as possible. But with her so close and yet so far, I can’t stop the questions. “So, how have you been?” Have you set any boys on fire lately? Burned down any schools this week? It’s my first chance to look at her. Really look at her – in all the weeks since we were together. There’s something bugging me about her but I can’t figure out what it is.

“Good. And you?” She’s not revealing much. Can’t read her body language.

“Same.” I get my papers from my bag. “I wrote down the lyrics to the song for you.” Then I realize what’s been nagging at me. “You look different.”

That cracks her reserved composure. A hint of the familiar unsettled, fragile Leila as she messes with her face, her hair, her clothes. “What do you mean? How different?”

I don’t bother trying to hide the fact that I’m studying her full-on now. “I don’t know. Just different.” Our eyes meet, catch and I get that sick feeling in the pit of my stomach. The dangerous feeling. Not good. I look away. Down at the ground. Anywhere but into those eyes that might read way too much. And that’s when I see it. The black patterning that edges her knees. A malu. She’s got a malu! The girl who said she was freaked at the mere mention of needles has now got a traditional Samoan tattoo that covers the top length of both legs. I can’t believe it. Disbelief. And yeah, maybe anger too. Betrayal. “Is that a malu?”

She sits up straight and immediately grabs at her skirt, trying to pull it down to cover the tell-tale markings. “Um yeah.”

“You got a malu done? When? Why? I thought you said you would never get a tattoo?” I thought I knew you. I was wrong. Even this most basic of details I would have bet my life on. And even that was wrong. You’re a dumbass Daniel. Can’t you get it? You don’t know anything about this girl.

The rest of the conversation is a dim haze while she tells me about getting her malu done. We talk about her fire. Her mother. About Maleko. And then we wander too close to stuff that’s too deep. Too painful. It ends the same way our last in-depth conversation ended. With her telling me to stay away from her. “You don’t know where I’ve come from, what kind of family or mother I descend from, you don’t know all the things I’ve done. You don’t know what I’m capable of…I’m no good for you…”

She leaves – running from the classroom as if she’s scared I’m going to try and stop her.

****

School becomes a tense, torturous thing. Every day we have dance practise. Every day I have to sing my heart out while Leila dances the siva. Just when I think life can't get any worse. It does. Simone's text comes late one night while I'm doing weights in the workshop.

Simone – *She's my friend. But u were my friend first.*

I don't have to ask who 'she' is. *What is it?*

Simone – *She's spending a lot of time with some palagi scientist from America. His name's Jason. Says they R just friends. Last weekend they went to the beach. Snorkelling. Tourist stuff.*

So that's who the blonde dude in the red truck is. *Images. Leila and Jason. Swimming together. Laughing together. She's in a skimpy bikini. He's got his arm around her waist as they walk into the sunset. Together.* Fury. It's thick, heavy and white-hot. I curse the empty night and slam my fist into the corrugated iron wall. Grateful my grandmother can't hear me from the house. *Get it together, man.*

I don't care if Simone doesn't believe my text back. *We're not together. She can go out with whoever she wants.*

The next day, I see him. The blonde scientist. He's parked at the front gate, standing by his truck. The whole world of Samoa College coconut wires sees Leila introduce him to Simone. And then the whole world sees her get in his truck and drive away. Together.

16

Culture Night is here. Everyone's buzzed. I'm already dressed in my gear. There's not much of it after all. Just a brief piece of brown *elei siapo* fabric tied low on my hips that stops mid-thigh. A bone carving necklace. And lots of coconut oil. Simone helped me with the oil and he went a little nuts. I'm a gleaming slick creature now – skin so slippery that I'm practically sliding along as I walk. I find an empty classroom so I can tune my guitar. Tune out the chaos so I can get calm before I go on stage later. I'm here to be alone so it's annoying when Mele walks in.

"There you are. I've been looking for you," she says gaily. "I wanted to see if you need any help with your costume." She comes over to where I'm sitting on a desk. Reaches out and runs her fingers lightly along my chest, down my arm. *What the hell?!* I put the guitar down and grab her hand before it can go any further. Any lower.

"No, as you can see, I'm all good. Thanks." You can go now.

She pouts. "Oh, I was looking forward to rubbing you down with coconut oil." She moves closer, to stand between my open legs, pressing her body against me. *Whoa*! She is seriously freaking me out now. I jump off the desk and push past her. She pulls at my hand to hold me back. "Where are you going?"

This has got to stop. Deep breath. Talk nice but firm. "Mele, I like you a lot. Any guy would be lucky to go out with you. But you and me? It's not gonna happen. Ever. Sorry."

Then before she can get mad/scream/slap me OR try to jump me again – I get my guitar and get the hell outta there.

****

Singing in front of an audience has never bothered me. I've been doing it since I was a kid and Mama had me up on the stand at church every White Sunday. Every time our pastor needed a soloist – she volunteered me. Every time our Village Women's Komiti needed entertainment for a fundraiser – they didn't even wait for Mama to volunteer me. Just put my name on the program. I'm sure there was a time when I used to be nervous. And dread the hushed crowd, the countless eyes on me. But Mama made sure I got over that shyness a long time ago. 'You have a gift from God and you must share that gift to show your gratitude.' Was her favourite line. Papa never argued with her on that. The two of them were always my greatest supporters. I'm grateful now that my grandmother forced me to perform so often. Because singing for a girl who doesn't want me – in front of an audience - is going to require all the composure I've got.

The crowd cheers as I walk out on stage. The lights dim. After the first few lines, the magic takes over like it always does and I get lost in it. Swept away in it. Midway through the song, the rest of the House joins in. That's her cue. Leila. My voice falters for a moment when I see her. Wearing the finery of a taupou – she is more than beautiful. She is majestic. Just what you'd imagine a warrior goddess to be. Her white siapo dress ends where her malu begins. Ancient markings chant of long ago. Oiled skin gleams. The burnished shell on her tall tuiga headpiece catches the moonlight as her eyes follow the flowing patterns of her hands. There is fierce strength in her dance. Sensual grace. Her face is alight. She is completely entangled in joy. Truly happy.

The world fades away and I sing to her. To only her. We are one in this prismed moment of color, sound and movement. It hurts when the song ends, when her dance comes to its close – because I want to hold this perfection in my hands. Breathe it in. Savor it. And never let it go.

****

It's late but Mama is waiting for me when I get home. There is beaming pride on her face as she hugs me, tells me how much she enjoyed my singing. She's made a pot of koko Samoa for us to share. Bitter sweet and rich. We talk. She asks me about Leila and I tell her everything. (Minus the fire explosion bits.) About the confusing past month. About tonight – my conversations with Leila in the truck, at McDonalds and outside her house. I tell Mama that even though me and Leila connected tonight, we parted on uneasy terms. Again. She pushed me away. Again. I tell Mama that yes, even though she warned me to stay away from Leila – I love her. And I don't know what to do.

Mama listens without interruption. When I am done, she reaches across the table and puts her hand on mine. "Tanielu, my heart aches for you. I can see you are hurting. I'm sorry. It doesn't matter what I think of this girl. What matters is how you feel. Your happiness means the world to me. Have you told her that you love her?"

"Of course not. She doesn't want me anywhere near her."

"Then my only counsel to you is – be a man. Own your feelings. Speak your heart to her. Hold nothing back. And if she does not accept it, then be a man and walk away, knowing that you will move on. You will find another one day, worthy of the gift you offer her."

I mull over her words late into the night. *Be a man. Own your feelings.* Could I do it? Could I be brave enough to 'speak' my heart and then accept whatever consequences came as a result? All I'm sure of is that I don't want to be stuck in confusion like this anymore. Leila can't keep screwing with me like this. It's time for me – and her – to make a choice.

I leave the house and start up the truck. I'm going to the pool. Our pool. Somehow, I know she'll be there.

Own your feelings. Speak your heart.

****

She's here. Black water and silver moonlight. It's a familiar scene – yet different. She's not the same girl. I'm not the same boy. We meet in the pool's center. We talk. I put it all on the line. Because this is the very last time I will tear open my chest and offer her all that I have to give. "I can be the waters that keep you real. Keep you focused. In tune, in control. We could do this, make it work, together. Tell me you don't want to give us a chance? Tell me you don't want to try? If you can look me in the eye and tell me honestly that you don't love me enough to try, then I promise, I'll leave this alone. I won't bother you anymore. And we can go on like – us – never happened."

Water, earth and sky are my witness – I speak my heart and every word, I speak true.

Leila whispers, "I love you, more than life itself."

Finally.

Water, earth and sky all shift into perfect alignment. And everything is right in the universe.

We move together. Her hands come up, clasping my face. There is an inferno in her eyes. Moonlight caresses the sleek lines of her lithe body. Just looking at her makes me hard – so hard it hurts. The most intense pleasure I've ever felt. I stroke my hands up her spine, melding her to me. Her fingers trace over my lips. I don't think. Just take her wandering finger into my mouth, sucking it. She makes a gasping sound. Shudders against me. Pulls her hand away. A tickled laugh escapes her. I've shocked her and she likes it. We kiss. I love the tart sweetness of her. Her tongue whispers across my lips. I open my mouth and allow her to taste me as I taste her. We're both teasing, taking, tasting. Her nails claw at my back. She's crushing her soft curves against me. I can feel everything. I want everything. My brain is on fire even more than my body – as I imagine her naked beneath me, her hair a riotous mass framing her face as she stares up at me with night-sky eyes, asking me, *willing* me to lick and taste her everywhere.

What am I doing?!

I release her. Back away. Stunned. How can a kiss be so intimate, so consuming? It's like we just had sex. Or something close to it. *Dammit. What the hell just happened?* "We better get you home. We shouldn't be out alone here, not if we're going to be doing this."

All the way to her house. All through our farewells. All the way back through the tangled forest to my truck. All the way back to my place. There's only one thing on my mind. Hammering at every painfully taut piece of me.

Sex.

I want to have sex with Leila. *No, that's not it.* I want to *make love* to Leila. Wild, gentle, fast, slow, untamed and precious sweet love to her.

But I can't. I shouldn't.

I won't.

*Say it a thousand times Daniel. Say it like you mean it. Scorch it into you - You will **NOT** have sex with Leila.*

No matter how bad you want her.

****

I can't sleep. In the painful quiet of my bedroom with a bed that I keep seeing Leila lying in. (Naked.) I give up chasing sleep and instead I make a list of all the things I won't do with Leila. Or else I might lose it and go where I shouldn't go. Do what I shouldn't do. My list looks a little something like this.

1. Don't be alone with her. Anywhere.
2. Don't kiss her with tongue.
3. Don't go swimming with her anywhere. Or engage in any other activity that requires her to take her clothes off. Don't take your clothes off around her either.
4. Don't touch her anywhere on her body that will turn you on. Like~~; her breasts, her cute ass, her neck (especially that dip where her pulse is), the curve of her shoulder, her hips, her legs (STAY AWAY FROM HER LEGS), her back - that ridged line of her spine, definitely do NOT suck on her fingers, the inside of her wrist – no, you can't kiss it, ever~~… Cancel all that. DO NOT TOUCH LEILA ANYWHERE ON HER BODY. AT ALL.
5. Don't think about sex when you're around her. Think about world peace, baby seals, starving children in Africa, calculus, the Pastor's sermon on 'The Sins of the Flesh'. And Maleko doing his Justin Bieber impersonation.

That last tip? Thinking of Maleko the Belieber? Works like a charm. Fastest way to put you off any kind of appetite.

17

What do you do when the girl you love more than life itself – is best friends with a man who's in love with her?

I'll tell you what I do. I grin and bear it.

We're here at the hospital with the antidote that Mama helped make. Leila's friend, the volcano scientist is lying on the bed. He looks awful. He's barely breathing. Not moving. Washed out and his skin looks grey. Up close, he looks real young. Not old at all. I thought he was supposed to be some old Professor, much older than Leila. Now he just looks very frail and very alone. It's not hard to believe that he's dying.

Leila convinces everyone to leave her alone in the room with him. I go too. He's a stranger to me – and I'm guessing he doesn't want a total stranger staring at him while he's knocked out cold.

When she finally comes out of the room, she looks even more miserable than when she walked in. Hope is getting crushed slowly but surely by the misery of reality. But she's not giving up. Not yet. I can see the resolve in her as she uses my phone to make the call. The one that will seal her fate. Everyone's fate – if Nafanua's coven are to be believed.

'Nafanua, it's me. Leila….'

I can't hear what Nafanua is saying but I don't need to. Leila's whole body is tensed. She's gripping the phone so tight her fingers are white. And when she gets off the phone, she's shaking. I hate that there is only so much I can do. So much I can offer. She's carrying a burden that I can't share. Her shoulders slump. Dejection. If I didn't hate Nafanua before this – I do now. Her threats are doing this to the girl I love. I take her in my arms. Frustrated. Wishing there was more I could do. I comfort her. But words of encouragement are only that – just words. "As long as we're facing this together, we will be alright. I'm not afraid, as long as I have you."

A lie. Because I ***am*** afraid. Of losing her.

The night drags. We sit and wait. The night drags. We sleep a little. Hospital benches suck. And then one of the palagi friends is shaking us awake. "He's waking up. Come see."

Leila is up in a flash. Out of my arms and down the hall. By the time I get to the door of Jason's room, Leila is standing by his bed. He's awake. His eyes are a brilliant blue. And they're staring up at my girlfriend with undisguised joy. He's not some washed out, frail palagi nerdy scientist anymore. No. He's stronger, he's smiling. And while I stand there in the doorway, he kisses her hand. *WTF*?! And then he speaks, "I wasn't joking, Leila. They tell me I've been dying for the last three days. And trust me, I felt like it. But you know the one thing that kept me hanging on? The one thing I kept fighting for?"

I know what the answer is before he says it. Because it would be mine if I were in his shoes. (Or in his hospital bed. He's not wearing any shoes…) And it's that realization that is the only thing stopping me from punching a hole in the wall right now. Oh yeah, and because it's seriously uncool to beat up people when they're recovering from knocking on death's door.

"You. And my promise to you." I knew it. He's in love with her. And I just helped save his life. Just great.

Leila's crying. I can tell. "Jason, no…" I want to get the hell out of there but I can't. I'm frozen in place because I want to know what she's going to say. I need to know. Is this where she wakes up to the realization that she's crazy in love with this volcano man and his ocean blue eyes? Is this where she turns to me and says, *sorry Daniel, I have to listen to my heart. And my heart is screaming Jason's name?*

He's still talking. Why can't he shut up already? "No, please, let me finish. Let a critically ill dude speak. Please?"

Yeah Leila, let him speak. We all want to hear this. Not.

"Leila, you asked me to be your friend. And nothing else." That's news to me. It's good news, right? I'm reeling here. Trying to stay upright but the world is determined to knock me over. "And I am. But nearly dying does something to a person y'know? It makes him realize that life is short. And you have to grab at every moment, every happiness with both hands. Tight. And not let go."

I'm going to grab onto his neck. Tight. And not let go.

"So yes, I'm your friend and I'm one hundred percent committed to helping you deal with your problem. But you gotta know…"

Here it comes. Here it comes. Wait for it. Brace yourself. You must not beat up an invalid. You must not beat up a man in a hospital bed.

"I'm in love with you Leila."

I knew it….I wonder if she knows I'm standing right here. And then I'm sure she knows. Because she tries to shut him up. "Jason, no, you don't know what you're saying. You're sick. You need to rest. Listen to your nurses." She's covering for him. Trying to salvage something from the wreckage. But what? My heart? My pride? Or his?

For a critically ill dude, he sure is tough to shut up. "I've never been more sure of anything in my whole life. I've loved you from that first night you bewitched me with your fake bimbo-ness. And then when I watched over you as you slept during that storm, then I was sure."

You. Slept. With. Leila. During a storm?!

The words hit me where I don't want them to. Low. In the gut. Everybody in the room heard him. Leila heard him. The palagi friends heard him. The nurses heard him. (They're rolling their eyes at the love drama. Samoan nurses at the National hospital are not known for their sensitivity or patience with people's feelings.) Everybody just heard him declare his undying love for my girlfriend. Everybody now knows that he's been in love with her since forever. And oh yeah, by the way, they spent the night together too.

I'm either the world's dumbest boyfriend. Or this volcano scientist's mind is seriously screwed up from telesa poison.

.

We leave the ward together. I've got nothing to say. Nothing calm and nice to say anyway. We get to the parking lot. It's dark. Making our way carefully through shadows. I open the passenger side door for her. She hesitates. Looks up at me. Silver moonlight on her face. She's worried. Questioning. She's wearing one of my old shirts and a lavalava. Her hair is pulled up into a tangled knot. She's a weary mess but she's never been more breath-taking. She's waiting for me to say something. Wanting to see if I'm mad. But I'm not going to play that game. I can be cool enough to be cool with my girlfriend's male friends. I am *so* cool like that.
"So, the antidote worked." I smile at her. Hoping she's convinced.

"Yeah, it seems like it."

"I'm glad." In that moment I really mean it. She cares about this Jason person. Enough to put her life on the line for him. If he means that much to her then I'm going to grin and bear it.

"I'm glad. I know he means a great deal to you. I'm glad." See? I said it twice. I'm glad. True story.

She smiles and I know I've made the right move. "Really? Even though…ummm…"

I tease her to let her know she's off the hook. "Even though the guy's crazy in love with you? Yeah, I'm still glad the antidote worked. Now if he hadn't been sitting on death's doorstep? Let's just say that I wouldn't have been so patient about standing by and watching some genius Professor hold your hand and profess his love for you. Or kiss you. I might have given in to the temptation to smash him. Or something like that."

Maybe there isn't enough fun in my voice because she winces. Gets that slightly hunted, fretful look in her eyes again. I hate to see her worried about anything. I pull her to me. Hold her close. "Seriously? I don't like it that Jason is in love with you. But he can help you in ways that I can't. And he's your friend." I look down into her eyes, letting just an edge of doubt creep into my voice. "That is all he is, right? Unless you do, have other feelings for him?" Stop it Daniel. You sound pathetic. Stop it.

But then she answers me in the best possible way. She stands on tiptoe, leans into me and kisses me. And it's not a soft, delicate kiss either. Adrenaline goes nuts, heartbeat rages. My list of good intentions combusts.

After everything that's happened in the last twenty-four hours – I don't want to hold back anymore. I want to erase every reminder of Jason. Every touch of him on her skin. Purge his declaration of love with pure unadulterated need. I'm kissing her. Pressing into her body. I'm lifting her up against me, wrapping her legs around me. She is soft everywhere that I am hard. And then I'm not thinking about Jason anymore. All I feel, all I want, all I need – is Leila. I want there to be nothing between us. Her breasts are crushed against my chest, soft and inviting. I want more. Of her. Of us. Of this. Her shirt is a nuisance. I push it out of the way so I can taste her. Pulse of throat, dip of shoulder, ridge of collar bone. Bite. Suck. Her skin is salty-sweet in the steaming hotness of the night. Valleys. The swell of her breast in my hand is a delight. Intoxicating. Her nipple pebbles under my fingers. An answering, surging hardness in my groin. More. I want more. Mouth follows hands. Tongue follows rivulets of sweat. Down. Curve, swell of flesh. I take her ripe fullness in my mouth. Soft moans in the darkness tell me she likes it. Wants it. As much as I do. I am lost in a swirling tide of wanting. Needing.

Leila. Ever since that night I first saw her in a forest pool of diamond-speckled darkness, I have dreamed about her. There, I have burned with her. Delighted in her. In my dreams I have her in all the ways I can't in reality. There, beside a vast ocean of raging wildness, she looks at me with eyes filled with white lightning as I claim her, slide into the tight sheathe of her. There, we bring each other to completeness in a song as ancient as the molten earth and the starlight that bathes us.

All of that happens with Leila. ***There***. In my fervid dreams where we both say yes.

But this is ***here***. Now. In the hospital parking lot. Where we should both be saying No. No. No. From somewhere far away, the word registers. A cold deluge of awareness. No. Don't do this. Not here. Not now. Not like this.

Stop.

Because it wouldn't be right. Because we can't. We shouldn't. It's the toughest thing I've ever done. Pulling away. When every serrated edge of me says yes.

But I do it. I stop. Hold her at a distance. We're both breathing fast. I need air. Distance. Space. It doesn't help when she pouts. Looks at me with that pleading expression on her face. "Daniel?"

She's all flushed. Hair a wildness of longing. Her clothes in disarray. Her lips have a swollen fullness about them. Ripe. Lush. Tantalizing me with wanting. Everything about her screams- ***sex.*** Screams - ***take me!***

And I want to.

"I'm sorry." I try to put her shirt back in place. Carefully. Trying not to touch her skin. "I shouldn't have done that. I'm sorry."

She closes the space between us. "I'm not sorry."

She holds me close. I don't dare breathe. Or move. I am a heartbeat away from knifing my resolve, from grabbing her and ripping her clothes off. I look down at her. There's a thin sheen of sweat on her neck, on the dip of her shoulder. Diamonds of longing in the night. I want to lave my tongue along her skin. Tasting. I want so many things. That I can't have. Not now. Not like this.

Her words are soft in the darkness. Pleading. "I love you. All I want is to be with you. What's wrong with that?"

Nothing. And everything. I think about the mother I never knew. A body washed up on a lonely shoreline. I think about my grandfather, the serious intent in his eyes when he told me to '*always treat women with utmost respect and honor.*' I think about my grandmother and her trust in me. Her hopes for me. I think about this girl, right here in front of me, right now. How much I love her. How much she means to me. I think about spending forever. With her.

I think of all these things - and I know I am doing the right thing. I'm making the right choice. "Nothing. But what I said back at the house? About respecting you enough to not put your virtue in question? I meant it. Just now, that – us getting carried away – it won't happen again. I promise. I'll be more careful. You can trust me. Okay?"

She looks at me with hurt in her eyes. Maybe she's disgusted with me. Now that I've shown her just how bad I want her in every physical sense of the word. Guilt is like bitter turmeric and black pepper. One of Mama's infamous tonics. You messed up Daniel. "We should get going. I need to take you home."

I turn away. Go to my side of the truck. Every step is an ache. Because I want to take her in my arms again. I get in. Still feeling the weight of what must surely be her disappointment in me. Her anger. She gets in across from me and the space between us feels like an endless chasm. I drive. Wishing I hadn't kissed her that way. Wishing I hadn't lost control even for a moment. Cursing hormones. Cursing lust. Cursing everything that makes me want her.

But then, she unhooks her seat belt and moves so she's sitting beside me. I almost drive off the road. I don't think I'm strong enough to say no to her again. But all she does is lean up to whisper against me, "I love you Daniel. Thank you for being worried about my ummm...virtue." The butterfly touch of her lips against my cheek. "I'll wait for as long as it takes. Until it's the right time for us."

And then she lays her head on my shoulder, nestles into me. A deep sigh that echoes in the truck. It sounds happy.

We drive the rest of the way like that. I think I know now what true contentment feels like.

It feels like the girl you love, falling asleep on your shoulder - with her heart, body and soul in tune with yours.

18

It's past noon before I wake up. And only because Mama comes in and yanks the curtains open. The light hurts my eyes. Still so tired. Late nights at the hospital have that effect on me. "Aaaargh…have mercy Mama!"

"I already did. I let you skip church." Is her pert response. "I need you to get up and make the saka of boiled bananas. You invited Leila over for dinner, remember? Unless you want to feed her bread and jam, then you better get up now."

"Okay, okay. I'm coming."

When she leaves me in peace, I lay there for a minute thinking about the day before. Meeting your girlfriend's family for the first time is supposed to be nerve-wracking but yesterday had been that and more. I'd never seen a group of women more beautiful than Leila's mother and aunts. Or more cruel. Sarona had been a nightmare and a half. I want to go ten rounds in the ring just thinking about what she did to Leila…

Mama and I work well in the kitchen together. Today she preps the fresh vegetables from our garden for the oka while I fillet the fish with expert ease and think about the night before. Me and Leila. Making out in the parking lot. The taste of her. The feel of her. The sound of her. Her breathless moan in the darkness. *Uh-oh.* Okay, maybe thinking about kissing Leila isn't such a good idea.

Especially not when I'm cooking in the kitchen with my grandmother. Time to think of something else!

Nafanua and her threats. Okay. That's enough to stifle even the most determined of hard-on's. What are Leila and I going to do? I sneak a glance at Mama. I'm going to have to tell her. The full story. I'm not looking forward to it. Because I keep remembering her warnings to me the day she first met Leila. Telling me to stay away from her. That she would be only trouble for me. And now, six months later, we are drowning in trouble. I love Mama. So much. I hate to think she could be in danger now. Because of me and Leila. *Mental note: get the welding team to camp out at the workshop for the next week. Just for extra security. For the times I have to go out anywhere.*

"Right, the oka is ready, marinating in the fridge. Now I just need to make the custard for the *puligi* pudding cake." Mama efficiently takes stock of our kitchen efforts. Before she can give me my next assignment though, the phone rings. It's one of the families that often comes to Mama for help. Their little girl is sick with a fever. Can Mama come see her please?

She gathers her supplies with the same quiet speed she employs in the kitchen and leaves, throwing final instructions over her shoulder. "You and Leila might need to have dinner without me." She hesitates in the doorway, giving me a look that speaks volumes. "Set the table outside in the garden."

I blow her a kiss. "Don't worry. I won't have Leila in the house without you here. There'll be no teenagers getting pregnant in this house today!" I tease her with the reminder of her mortifying mistake the previous day and she gives me an unwilling smile.

"Don't be cheeky son. Toetiti salapu oe, eh!"

I watch her get into her little car and drive away. It will be just me. And Leila. Dining alone. For the first time. For a split second I catch a glimpse of a future where we have dinner together. All the time. In our own little house somewhere.

Forever looks good with Leila in it.

The same bubbly feeling lingers as I set the table out in the garden with a Sunday best tablecloth and dishes. Hmm, Mama is better at this then I am but I have a ridiculous urge to make everything look good. Special. I want to impress her. Make her light up. I get some coconut candles for the centrepiece. Pick some white gardenia. I can't find a vase so I grab a huge abalone shell and stick the flowers in there. Not bad. Maybe I've got some interior décor skills after all. Everything looks good. What else do we need? Aha, music. Of course. I get the stereo set up with some sounds. The sun is doing its final blaze up before it sets. By the time she gets here, it will be nice and cool there in the garden shadows. I dish up the food and carry it to the table outside.

When the woman speaks from somewhere behind me, it's a shock and I almost drop the bowl of oka. "Isn't this pretty!"

I turn. It's Sarona. Right here in our garden. She's got two other sisters with her. And they're all smiling – but not in a good way. Oh shit. There's three very pissed off telesa spirit women in our garden and I'm standing here holding a bowl of chopped fish. Great. Just great. I put the bowl down on the table. Ask, "What do you want?"

I'm keeping calm on the outside, but on the inside – I'm racing through all my possible options. Anyone who's ever lived in Samoa knows that calling the police is not a viable option. Not if you want speedy response action anyway. Besides, I didn't think they would be very useful against a trio who chuck lightning at people. Of one thing I'm certain – I need to get them away from here before Mama comes back. Before Leila shows up.

Sarona steps closer, still smiling that freaky smile, "Is that any way to greet family?"

She doesn't give me time to debate semantics, putting on a syrupy sweet, breathy voice, "I mean if you and Leila are eternal lovers – why then that makes us related. Just call me Aunty Sarona."

All three of them laugh. Twisted, sick bitches. Sarona continues, "We're here because the Sisterhood wants to get to know you a little better, don't we ladies?" More snide laughter. "We need to talk."

I give them my bored but irritated face. The one I use for rotten little third formers who cause a ruckus in assembly. The one that says, *You are so pathetic that I won't even waste anger on you.* "Fine. So talk."

Sarona shakes her head. "Oh no, not here. We're taking you with us. To chat somewhere else a little more…private."

"And if I don't want to go?"

No more smiles now. "You misunderstand me. This is not an invitation. We are taking you with us. Now."

Anything to get them away from here. "Okay, let's go then."

The three of them part ranks, motioning for me to walk ahead first. "Go on. We have a car out front."

I walk down the pebbled pathway, through soft lush hues of color, around the side of the house with the women following closely behind me. I stop in the front driveway. *Whoa*. There's a badass silver Porsche Panamera Hybrid in front of our house. I didn't think you could even get those in the Pacific…but now is not the time to get excited about a car.

Choices. To my right across the yard, is my truck. With the keys in the ignition. I could be out of here in a heartbeat. Find a phone to warn Leila and Mama. Meet up with them somewhere. Figure out where to go. What to do. But I hesitate. Because across the black strip of tar seal is the seawall and the beckoning blue. The ocean.

For some strange reason, the sapphire water calls to me. It thinks it's an option. I don't know why. What am I going to do? Swim away from them?!

Behind me, Sarona reproves sharply, "Hurry up, what are you waiting for? Move it."

I'm in a confusing scrum of emotions. Because if they were three MEN shoving me around, I would have no doubts about what to do. No hesitation about turning, tackling one and then getting up to throw punches at the other two. I've taken on worse on the field. But this is different. This is three WOMEN. And I don't hit girls. Papa was always very clear on that. *We don't hit women. Ever. No matter how angry we feel, no matter how badly they hurt us. A man never raises his voice or his hand to a woman.* I should have asked him if that applied to demon women with trigger happy elemental powers. I saw what Sarona did to Leila yesterday. I know what she could do to me today.

Speed and unpredictability are what I'm known for on the rugby field. I need them now. I need them bad. I make my decision. Split-second choice. I bend, grab a handful of sand, turn, throw it in Sarona's face and then run for the truck.

Enraged scream, "Aargh, my eyes! Somebody get him."

I don't look back to see who's going to obey her. I'm at the truck, wrenching open the door when the first strike hits me. The world lights up, a blinding flash, a loud crackling sound rips through me. Deafening. Blinding. It hurts. Shit, it hurts. More than a dozen rucks. This is like a meat shredder going through my insides. It brings me to my knees. It shames me that I'm so easily dropped. As fast as it hits, the lightning strike ends. Leaving me weak. Still hurting. I'm on all fours in the sand now. I shake my head, trying to clear the haze of pain. I hear them laughing.

"Not so tough now, are you big boy?"

There are sandaled feet to my right. Red nail polish and diamante toe rings. You know my brain isn't working properly if I can fixate on such an inane detail at a time like this. *Get it together Daniel.* I send my Papa a prayer, asking for his forgiveness. *Sorry Papa.* I reach, grab at one ankle and yank her off her feet. Then I'm up, standing – swaying but standing. Gotta get away. I can't see properly but it doesn't matter. There's two more hazy shapes standing in my way, blocking my path to the truck. I give up on the truck and turn to make for the ocean. In my head I'm running but the sorry fact is that I'm only staggering, every step rips me up inside. Can anything hurt more than this?

Yes.

A woman shouts, "Take him down. Enough playing around." I hear a rushing sound that builds from faraway. Like a jet plane taking off. A crazy construction site of bulldozers on hyper drive. And then it hits me. A cannonball of wind. All the air is knocked out of me. I'm off my feet, spinning. In a furious channel of air but none of it for breathing. I'm suffocating, dying. And then I slam into something. Hard. I fall. Face down in the dirt.

It's my workshop. Hitting an aluminium siding wall at sixty miles an hour is a bitch. I thought getting taken down by Malua was bad. This is a thousand times worse. Every bone in my body feels it. A cup of dice rattled...shaken not stirred… and then chucked on the ground. My mouth is full of gravel. I spit it out, tasting blood. Oh shit, is that a piece of tooth?

The one good thing about the wind slam? It erases my hang-ups about hitting women. All bets are now off. Bitches – I'm ready to rage. I get up, trying not to count how many ribs might be cracked. Push on. Push forward. Push through the pain. Push. Sarona and her tag team are walking towards me. Still laughing. Triumphant. Clearly this is how they get off. Wiping the floor with testosterone. They're blocking my escape route to the beach and the truck. At my back is the workshop. I sidle along the wall, feeling blindly with my hands behind me for the doorway handle, not taking my eyes off the Sisterhood. They're taking their time. Why not – they have me cornered. And they've got an arsenal of air magic at their fingertips. I'd relish it too if the situations were reversed.

I find the handle for the door. Got it! Jerk it open, push and half fall backwards into the workshop, jamming the door after me. There's no lock. I've never needed one before. Jam a piece of scrap metal underneath the door, knowing it will only be a temporary barrier for them. Hoping it buys me enough time. I go to the storeroom of all my gear.

Outside, Sarona's mocking cry is loud and clear, "Come out, come out little boy. Come out and play!"

How many times can you call someone a bitch in your head before it becomes redundant? Not enough times. I find what I'm looking for – the portable blowtorch. I belt it on, securing the straps for the mini gas bottle on my shoulders. Am I scared? Yes. But rage is stronger than fear. There's a massive crash as they hit the metal doors with something. Probably a blast of wind. The entire building rattles. Again, another blast. This one stronger than the first, has the steel beams grating. Again the invitation, "Daniel Tahi, you're being a very naughty boy. Come out here now."

The roller doors buckle. Like a giant fist has punched a hole in them. I take up my position towards the back of the workshop, behind a stacked pile of steel rafters. Waiting. The doors give way, fly and hit the back wall. I can't see them from where I'm hiding but I can hear them. "Where is he? Fotu go check outside the back in case he went out a back door. Quickly."

The sound of feet running lightly over the gravelled coral as someone called Fotu obeys. That leaves two of them. In here with me. I brace myself. Fingers ready on the trigger mechanism. Wait, wait, wait. Wait for them to get close. Not until they're almost on me, not until then do I move. I switch the blowtorch on, turn around the corner of the steel rafters. The blue flame sears the first woman on the shoulder. They both scream, stumble back. I'm wielding the blowtorch like a flame thrower now, spraying cobalt fire everywhere, creating a shield between me and them. I want to stand here and set fire to them both, watch them crisp. (What can I say, I'm only human.) But it's only a fleeting wish. I've unsettled them, bought myself some time, an escape space. They'll have to burn another day.

They're covering their faces, coughing and spluttering. There's smoke everywhere, the sharp bite of acetylene. They're choking on fumes. Sarona recovers first. She grabs a loose pipe, swings it at me. I duck. Drop the blowtorch and tackle her. We go down on the concrete in a scrabbling heap. I'm on top of her. I should hit her. Pound her with my fists. But I can't do it. Even now, even after all they've done, I can't bring myself to punch a woman in the face, especially not when she's down and fragile-looking. *Yes, I am being stupid.* And I pay for it. In that moment of hesitation, she hits me with a blast of lightning that crackles and rips from fingertips to my face. It knocks me back away from her. Blinds me. My eyes are black with pain. Burning coals shoved in my eyes. Somebody's screaming. It takes a moment to realize that it's me.

I'm clawing at my eyes, trying to stand. I see dim shapes. Sarona picks up the pipe again. Swings. Connects. With my ribs. Thank you for breaking the few unbroken ribs I had left. So nice of you not to leave any unloved. She's yelling, cursing, bitching. I don't care. Because everything hurts so bad now. I'm mad at myself. *You idiot. You should have beat the shit out of her when you had the chance…now look where you're at.* I get to my feet. I gotta get out of here. Move Daniel. Move. Get away. Hands claw at me, ripping my shirt as I stagger out of there. Keep moving. I'm outside. Start running for the truck. And then stop. Because my grandmother's car has just pulled up to the house. She looks at me. Her face is afraid, questioning. I shout, "Go Mama, quick! Get away from here."

Even as I say the words I know she won't listen. She's the only mother I've ever known. She loves me more than life itself. She's not going anywhere. Instead she gets out of the car, starts coming towards me. "Daniel? What happened? Are you alright?"

I feel them come up behind me. Sarona and her tag team. "Look who's come to join the party. Is this your grandmother Daniel?"

I don't move. Together we watch as Mama takes a few steps forward and then stops, her eyes narrowing as she makes sense of the situation. She speaks and she's the stern, authoritative woman that would tell me off when I needed it, "What are you doing with my boy?"

"This is telesa business. Daniel needs to come with us. Or else Nafanua will kill both of you."

Sarona whispers the rest low, so that only I can hear it. "You leave with us or we lightning strike the old woman. Make your choice and make it fast."

There is no choice to be made here. "Leave my grandmother alone. Let's go."

"Wise decision." She calls out to Mama. "Stay back old woman." For extra emphasis she sears a line of fire down the ground in front of us, drawing a line that must not be crossed.

"Bitch" I hiss. "Don't do anything to hurt her. We have a deal. I'll go quietly. Let her go."

Mama doesn't look afraid. If anything she is mega-pissed off. She doesn't move but she calls out. "I am the daughter of Tavake. That is my son gifted to me by the Covenant Keeper. You take him and you will answer to her."

I have no clue what she's talking about. But it's clear that the telesa do because they look shaken, exchange glances loaded with meaning. One whispers, 'Do you think Nafanua knows?"

Sarona only hesitates for a minute, "It doesn't matter. Tonga is far away. Tavake has no voice here. Let's go. Get him in the car."

With a line of fire marking me as theirs, grandmother watches as the women take me to the Porsche. Before I get in, they hit me with one more electric strike. Because they want me to feel extra welcome and beloved. This one has me on my knees in the dirt, retching. I get some on Sarona's shoes and it makes me feel perversely happy. I hope I puke up again in their swanky car.

They put me in the trunk and shut me in darkness. The car starts and jerks into motion. It hurts. Every bump and jostle as the car takes to the road hurt. The pain reminds me I've been electrocuted and windbitch-slapped. It feels like they're hitting every pothole on purpose. In the stifling darkness, I feel my ribs. What's left of them. I'm taking shallow breaths because it hurts otherwise. They turn on the stereo. Loud. The bass pulsates in the trunk. *Like I don't already have a headache.* It's Beyoncé's 'Girls Run the World' song. Their twisted sense of humor no doubt. Just brilliant. They're evil *and* wannabe-comedians too.

Every man should get beat up by a Telesa Sisterhood at least once in their life. Because I guarantee you will never doubt the power and strength of a woman ever again. (You're supposed to laugh at that. Because I'm too sore right now to laugh at my own lame jokes.)

I settle in for the ride, shutting my eyes against the throbbing pain in my head, my side, my chest.

But the worst pain of all is the one in my heart. I failed. I didn't escape. I didn't warn away the ones I love. I didn't protect them.

Where are they taking me? Where's Leila?

19

We drive for a long time. I may even have dozed off. Staying alert is proving difficult. It's stuffy in the cramped space. I'm glad when the car finally stops moving. I wanted to come out of there raging as soon as they opened the trunk but instead I only do a kind of floppy stumbly thing and end up on the ground again with my face in the sand. Maybe they'll just let me lie here. Then I can clear my head. Find a way to block out the pain that's steadily throbbing away. Like a rap soundtrack that just won't shut up. The ocean is nearby. Crickets chat in the evening. Women are talking. There are more voices than the Sarona trio. I recognize Nafanua's but the others are unfamiliar.

"Sarona and I will go get Leila. The rest of you restrain him. Wait for us."

Leila. That's all I need to block out the pain that's threatening to drown me. Footsteps. Some people leave. A car starts up and drives away. Rough hands pull at my wrists. A sharp voice, "Pass the rope. We'll tie him up before he gets any ideas."

No. Nobody's tying me up. Nobody's going to hurt Leila. They've half-tied my hands when I jerk them away. Roll. Shift. Scramble to my feet. Shaking off the restraint. Quick look around. We're in a sandy clearing. Trees. Beach to my left. Bush to my right. That's all I have time for. Hands grab me from behind. Move. Act. Now. So what if it hurts. I elbow the one behind me, uncaring that it's a she. Uncaring of the half-strangled sound she makes as she falls back. There's another woman directly in front of me. Get her before she lightning strikes you. I backhand her across the face. Cringing inside as I do. *Papa forgive me.* She goes down. Where's the other ones? There's got to be some more of them.

A familiar crackling sound announces her presence. I turn. There's a woman with blonde streaked hair in a ruffled pink island print dress standing there. Her hands are lit up fireballs of energy. She looks mega-pissed. The face and the fizzy hands don't match her frilly outfit at all. *Oh hell.* She aims a line of sparks at me. A blazing whip of light. I sidestep. It usually works better on the rugby field. But then usually I don't have several broken ribs. Most of the lightning whip misses me. But the flicker lash that does whisper against my shoulder, serrates the flesh. Blood gushes. I ignore it. Spin around, duck another whiplash and take her down with a full body slam tackle. We roll over rocks and sand. She's kicking and screaming and biting. We come to rest against a fallen tree trunk. I grab hold of her and pull us both up to a standing position, so she's got her back to me. There's a piece of rope still attached to one of my wrists. I hook it over her head, around her neck. Chokehold. Her struggling eases. There are three other Telesa arrayed before us in the clearing. All wearing impeccable skin-tight dresses. Vibrant slashes of color in the night. Emerald green. Sunburst yellow. And passionfruit purple. They are the angriest looking bunch of pretty women I've ever seen. I tighten my grip. I say the words rough against her ear. "Call them off or I'll kill you."

I hope she believes me. Because I don't.

She's frozen in my arms. Drawing in ragged frenzied breaths. Hands at her throat. But at least she's not struggling. She's my ticket out of here. I yell at the others. "Back off. I want the keys to the car. Or I'll snap her neck."

We start moving towards where the cars are parked. A couple of Land Cruisers and the Porsche. I'm not taking my eyes off the three in front of me. I have a plan. It involves me getting in a car *with* a fully loaded lightning strike sister *without* getting fried and then racing to get Leila before her mother does. I hope I get points for trying.

Because trying is as far as I get.

The Sister in yellow smiles at me. A flick of her wrist and a massive line of fire scissors from the sky. Not at me. But at a black Land cruiser. Which obliges her by blowing up. An incendiary explosion of sound, light and heat. The fallout knocks me off my feet, jostles my grip on the pink Telesa and once again, I'm face first in the dirt. Over the crackling sound of flames and burning metal, I hear women laughing.

I hate that sound so much.

I get up. The pink Telesa has scrambled away from me. Now I'm facing off against four Telesa. I've got no hostage. No weapons. No escape route. Nothing. I don't have much time to feel sorry for myself because Pink Telesa wants me to know that she doesn't appreciate being put into a chokehold. No sir. "How dare you put your hands on me and threaten my life? I am Telesa. I am Matagi. I am earth. And you. Are. Nothing."

Uh oh. She's got those flaming hands again. Only this time, there's matching sparks in her eyes. I turn to run but it's too late. A whip lash of pure energy rips across my bare back, taking skin with it. Before it even has time to register, she's whipped me again. Double ouch. Once again, I'm ashamed by how easy it if for them to bring me to my knees. My mind says, STAND UP. But my body refuses to obey. There's redness blurring my vision. A coiled wire of lightning rakes my chest now. Blood spatters on the sand. Is that mine?

She does the whip thing at me. Many times. So many times that I give up counting. I got nothing left. I'm in a convulsing heap in the dirt and my skin is on fire. A thousand stinging fire ants. Are marching relentlessly across my back. My legs.

I got nothing.

When darkness comes, it brings oblivion. I sink into it screaming.

Leila, wherever you are. Run.

****

There's razorblades methodically scraping my soul to pieces. In a regular rhythm. The darkness hurts. But the faraway light hurts even more. I fight it. No. I don't want to meet it. Let me stay here in this hole where I can die a little more in peace. From that faraway light I hear voices.

"Bring him out."

That must be the signal for me to wake up. I'm being dragged. I don't envy the ones doing the dragging. I'm no lightweight. And then they're chucking me on the ground. I want to vomit. But I don't have the strength. So I just lay there. And choke on it. Can I just die already? Please?

"Daniel? No, Daniel!" It's Leila. She's screaming. "What have you done to him? Daniel? Please answer me."

I want to answer. But I can't. *I love you. I'm sorry I couldn't do anything to stop this. I'm sorry I'm just a boy. No lightning in my spine. No wind at my fingertips. No fire in my bones. Just a boy.*

Leila's trying to bargain. Trying to save me. With words. It doesn't make sense. Why isn't she setting the place on fire? Why isn't she blasting them all to a fiery hell hole?

Sarona shuts her up. "Pathetic. See, sisters? This is why we don't give ourselves to men. See what happens? It makes us weak."

Lady, I don't know what man in his right mind would want you anyway. Trust me. We barely know each other and all I want to do is stab you in the throat while you sleep.

I'm trying to move. Sending messages to the jellified mess that used to be my body, *get up!* It's not listening. Surprise, surprise. The scorpion woman is still talking.

"You are supposed to be the most powerful telesa that has walked this land in over three hundred years and look at you. Reduced to tears and begging, for what? For this?" Something kicks at my side. *Ouch*. "Now, let's see what she does when I do this." And then I'm a seething mass of agony because she's zapping me again. It goes on forever. But this time it's worse because its mixed with the bitter shame of knowing that Leila can hear me scream. *Oh yeah, by the way, that guy you thought was tough-as? Smashing people left, right and center on the rugby field? Yeah, well he's not so good at handling getting his innards fried.*

Leila's begging now. "Please stop it. You're killing him. I'll do whatever you want. Just please stop it. Daniel!"

Death can't come fast enough. My one consolation? They're too busy ripping into me so they can't rip into Leila. It's a small comfort. But I hang on to it tight. I use it to help me to a kneeling position. The pain is steadying to a dull ache. Leila has stopped pleading. Instead her voice is calm and strong. "Nafanua, call off your dog. I am ready to be what you want me to. I am ready to do whatever it is that you want. Let him go."

This doesn't sound good. What does her mother want her to do? Leila's gotta know by now that she can't trust these women. I find my voice. It scrapes out over the rocks and knives and thorns that have taken up residence in my chest, in my throat. “Leila? What’s going on?”

I see her now. They’ve got her tied up to something in the water. Black ocean up to her chest. She looks mega-pissed. But otherwise unharmed. A relief. So they haven’t been cutting at her like they’ve been doing to me. Our eyes meet and she sends me a smile. “Daniel, it’s okay. Everything’s gonna be okay. I’m sorry I got you into this. Please forgive me.”

I can’t feel my legs anymore and there’s more blood caked on me then clothes. But there’s nowhere I’d rather be than right here. With her. So we’re probably going to die. In that moment, I accept that. And I’m okay with it. Because I would rather die alongside her than live without her. How do I make sure she knows that?

Sarona makes a gagging noise. “Oh please, enough. You two are sickening. Silence fool.” She does that sparking crackly move with her hands but I’m too exhausted to even flinch anymore.

Nafanua stops her before she can hit me again though. “Enough Sarona. See? Leila’s ready. We don’t need this boy anymore. Let him go.” She tells the others to cut Leila loose.

No way. I’m not going anywhere. I don’t have to argue because Sarona doesn’t think it’s a good idea either, “Are you crazy? We can’t let him go, not until she’s done what she’s supposed to.” I don’t get it. What do they want Leila to do? She told me about the factory incident at Vaitele. And how the Sisterhood wasted that village because of some whales. This is not some Women’s Komiti sisterhood that weaves mats and inspects gardens for rubbish. I’m scared for her. Scared for what they’re trying to make her do. They’re taking me down to the beach now where there’s a canoe creaking quietly in the pulsing tide. No. I don’t want to go. I have to stay here. As long as we’re together, I don’t care what happens.

“Let me go. Leila! Don’t you hurt her.” Struggling, trying to keep her face in my line of vision. Trying to forge a link, a thread that can't be broken. No matter what they do to us. They hit me with a lightning blast. Short, sharp and sweet. I fight it but it's no use.

Blackness. I sink into it with her face in my head. Clinging to the memory of her lips on mine. The feel of her, the taste of her, the smell of her. Leila.

I'm out.

****

I'm tangled in a web of darkness so thick it suffocates me. So heavy it crushes me. I push. Struggle. Fight. For Leila. I need to get out of here. I need to wake up. I need to push past the night, past the pain, past the chains. For Leila. From far away I hear her voice, "Don't you dare speak of my father that way, he was worth a thousand of you!"

There is the familiar searing sound of lightning and Leila's muffled sob. They're torturing her. I die inside, wishing I could take her pain. Wishing I could be her substitute on this battlefield. I open my eyes to a star filled sky.

The scorpion shouts, "Fouina, this fool needs a reminder why she has to show us respect. Cut him, now!" That can mean only one thing. I'm the only male on this beach. Here we go.

Rough hands jerk me up. I'm in a boat, out on the water but not too far away from the shore where the Telesa surround Leila. They've brought her to her knees. Moonlight reveals her tear-stained face, the anguished look she sends me. She screams, "No!"

One of the women grabs a fistful of my hair, yanks my head back. Ouch. The glint of steel. A knife slashes across my chest. The sting feels good. It lets me know I can still feel. I was worried I would never feel anything again. My body is still working. Even after all they've done to it. They chuck me back on to the bottom of the boat. There's wet stuff pooling where I'm lying. It takes a few minutes for me to realize that its blood. My blood. Lots of it. And it's not slowing. It's surging with every pulse beat of my heart. That beats its song for Leila.

Mine, mine, mine. You are mine and I am yours.

I am swimming now. In a blood-red pool. I'm losing it. Hallucinating. Mama's face looms. '*Daniel, you're making a mess with all that blood! Stop that right now. You need to be bandaged. Get up immediately.'* I try to tell her that it's not my fault. But her face fades into the redness. And my Papa is there instead.

'Daniel, you shouldn't hit a woman. Ever. It doesn't matter what they do or say to you.' Shame burns. Chokes. Or is that the blood gurgling in my throat? I don't know anything anymore. Papa is disappointed in me. So am I. Leila is suffering. And I can't help her. Mama is mad at me. So am I. Leila needs me. And here I am lying in a puddle of blood in a freakin' canoe.

I'm fading in and out of some peaceful place where nobody zaps you with energy bolts that fry your guts. Where nobody scores the skin off your back with razor whips of lightning. Where nobody carves you up with a knife just for kicks. That place is calling me. Tugging me with an inevitable force. But I can't go there.

Because Leila is still out here.

Out of the jumble of voices, one breaks through the dizzying fog. "Kill the boy. Now."

Yes, that would be me again. The boy.

I think I hear Leila saying 'No.' I wish she had said something else. That's the last thing I'll ever hear her say. ***'No'*** doesn't really bring a lot of comfort when you're about to depart for that long road to the other side you know. (Yeah, I know I'm still cracking jokes. Right up to the end. It gives me a perverse pleasure. Knowing that I'll die laughing inside.)

Hands raise me up. This time the blade doesn't dance along my chest. This time it sinks all the way in. Twists with a viciousness that takes me by surprise. The night stands still. Leila. She is screaming but I can't hear her.

Thoughts like swirling leaves in a storm of madness. Slipping out of my fingers. No matter how hard I try to catch them. Hold them. *Leila. I'm sorry. We will never sit down together for dinner. We will never hold hands across the table in our own home. I'm sorry.*

She is crying.

Be still my love. I am here. I will never leave you. I'm right here.

I wish it were true.

I fall. And as I fall, I take her with me.

Do you know what death feels like? As a million and one sparks of life flicker, dim and then are extinguished? Neurons die like butterflies scattering on the wind as they flutter their last breath. Your lungs release their final gasp of CO2. And your heart shudders to its concluding beat. And as consciousness slips away, you realize, death is sweet. Nothingness is joy. Better than living. Better than breathing. When you are without the purpose for your existence. Nothingness is joy.

I AM DANIEL TAHI.

20

Sand. Stars. Ocean. Moonlight. And Leila. What better way to wake up?

"Leila? Is that you?" Her skin gleams silver in the night. Her hair is unbound, loose waves are a lush waterfall of flecked sand. She's alive. She's here with me. Is she real? Or is this a dream? I am afraid. Because if it is a dream, then I don't want to wake up. Ever.

She lights up at the sound of my voice. "Hey, it's me. I'm here, baby. I'm here. You're okay. We're both okay." Tears glisten on her cheeks. Why is she crying if we're both okay?

I want to catch her tears. Touch her "Don't cry. You're the fire goddess remember? You don't cry."

She smiles and all is right in my world. This is the kind of dream I can live in. For an eternity. "Yeah, I do. Fire goddesses always cry when the one they love comes back from the dead."

"Who said I was dead?" I'm confused. I wasn't dead. I was swimming in an underwater palace where a mermaid woman smiled at me and called me a Silver Dolphin Prince. But yeah, that's not the kind of stuff you tell people. Not unless you want them to think you're on drugs.

I try moving. Is everything working? Not a good idea. The world spins and it's spiked with daggers of hurt. "Ouch. Last thing I remember they were zapping you with lightning and I couldn't do anything about it. I couldn't help you. Some boyfriend I turned out to be." I can't keep the bitterness out of my voice. How much more useless can I be?

She rushes to lie to me. Trying to make me feel better about being a loser. "Are you kidding? I'm the girlfriend with a psycho family. A family that stabbed you and threw you into the ocean for the sharks."

"They did? I don't remember that. So where are they?"

Her smile is replaced with a cold hardness. "Gone. All of them." She is rigid with tension. What has she done? I remember the school field blazing that night so long ago, the way she laughed at the flames.

"How did you do it? What happened? How did I get here?" I take a deep breath and sit up, bracing myself for the inevitable razorblade of pain. That's when I see her. REALLY see her. She's naked. From head to toe. Every delicious inch of her. The sight of her hits me hard. Look away, quick. "Ummm, Leila?"

"Yeah?"

"Did you know you were naked?"

She flushes, grabs at her hair like it's a curtain, folds her arms across her chest. "No, I'm not! I'm covered. A bit." She's flustered. Blustering. And there are tantalizing pieces of her peeking out from behind her flimsy covering. I love it. "We just escape from the jaws of telesa death and the first thing you do is notice my lack of clothes? Stop looking at me."

Happiness bubbles out. Relief. This is real. We're okay. We made it. I laugh, reach for her, hold her face in my hands. The mouth I thought I would never taste again. The eyes I thought I would never see again. She is real. She is okay. We made it.

You are mine. Mine, mine, mine. You are mine and I am yours.

“I’m not. Looking at your body, I mean.” A lie. Who could NOT look at her? Sinuous curves and supple lines of silver-edged mystery. “Because I’m too busy looking into your eyes. So I can make very, very sure – that this is for real. That you’re real. I thought we’d lost each other tonight.” And then I can’t hold back what I’ve been wanting to do since I first opened my eyes and found her beside me. We kiss. And it’s hungry and replete all at the same time. I fist handfuls of her wild hair, drawing her even closer. Her hands are on my chest, her touch sets my every nerve on fire. Heat surges inside me, deep and low. So hard it aches.

Ask me to define desire. It’s her. Leila. It’s sand, stars, rushing ocean, moonlight. And her.

I pull away. Or else I’m going to smash through all my own sexual codes of conduct... I try to smile, try to breathe. “Yes, you’re definitely real.” *Don’t look down. Don’t look down.* I look down. At her. All of her. “And you’re very naked.”

Outrage. More scrambling to cover something with nothing. “Daniel! You promised.”

She’s so incredibly cute like this, eyes going everywhere trying to find an escape route. Practically digging a hole in the sand for herself. I’m not helping. No way. This is more fun than I’ve had in a long time. Hey, cut me some slack - I’m a guy and I just got tortured and stabbed by a gang of psycho’s. “Sorry.” A lie.

“I can’t help myself.” Which is not a lie.

She chucks a threat at me. Which means nothing. “Don’t look. Or I’ll never speak to you again.” I just laugh, still enjoying the view. Memorizing every luscious detail. Just in case, I never ever get to relish in it again.

She's scrabbling in the sand. A whoop of triumph. She's found something. Dammit. A piece of rag that she wraps around her waist. Huge sigh of relief from her. *Aww, buzz killer*. She arranges her hair over her top half. Careful and precise – before she helps me to stand. "Come on, let's get out of here. You're hurt and I want Mama to take a look at you." She gives me a strange look. Questions in her eyes that she won't ask. Not now anyway. I'm feeling better by the minute. Especially with her pressed against my side, her arm looped around my waist as she tries to support my weight. The firm curve of her breast is nestled against my chest and she's threaded my arm through her hair, across her shoulders. This close she is warm, soft, inviting. The air tastes of her. Brown sugary caramel and a resounding hint of roasted cocoa bean. I love the way she feels. Smells. Tastes. We walk. Slowly. Across the beach. Towards the black lava rocks. There is a moon dying in the sky. The sea breeze plays on the desolate sand.

Leila pauses. She's looking out over the spread of rocks. She's sad. There's a crystal tear on her cheek. "Are you okay?" What did they do to her? What really happened here?

She shakes her head. "Yeah, I'm fine. Let's go." She's keeping her secrets. Can't blame her. We all have them.

I pull her close for a moment. Breathe deep with my face buried in her hair. I don't know why we've been given a second chance. Why we're still alive. Why we're here walking away from this beach, hand in hand. But I don't care. Because we're together. And that's all that matters.

Water, earth and sky are in perfect alignment. And everything is right in the universe

The End.

'Daniel and Leila' – Models, Faith Wulf and Ezra Taylor.

I AM DANIEL TAHI.

“Daniel Tahi”. Photographer, Jordan Kwan. Model, Ezra Taylor.

I AM DANIEL TAHI.

ABOUT THE AUTHOR

Lani was born and raised in Samoa. She received her tertiary education in the USA and New Zealand before returning home to work as a secondary school English teacher and writer. Her first book 'Pacific Tsunami- Galu Afi' is an account of the 2009 disaster that devastated islands in Samoa, American Samoa and Tonga. It weaves together the stories of survivors, rescuers, and medical/aid workers. It was commissioned by Hans Joe Keil and published with funding from the Australian Govt. Aid Program. Lani released the first book in the Telesa Series in October 2011 and the second in June 2012. She is currently working on the next in the series, The Bone Bearer, to be released in April 2013. Her collection of short stories, 'Afakasi Woman' won the 2011 USP Press Fiction Award. Lani is married to Darren Young and they have five children. She writes about life as a (slightly demented) Domestic Goddess at her blog: Sleepless in Samoa

4352820R00080

Made in the USA
San Bernardino, CA
14 September 2013